COLD CALLING
& OTHER STORIES

Pronounced unfit for frontline duty due to injury, and eligible to retire in a year, DS Fran Phoenix is given a new job heading up the cold cases team — or 'put in a corner' in the basement, as she sees it. Teamed up with a PC with barely two years' experience, they reopen the twenty-five-year-old case of a missing girl — but evidence continues to be thin on the ground. Can the oddly matched duo heat up the trail and uncover the truth? Three stories from the pen of Geraldine Ryan.

D0496358

GERALDINE RYAN

COLD CALLING
And Other Stories

Complete and Unabridged

LINFORD
Leicester

First published in Great Britain

First Linford Edition
published 2018

A catalogue record for this book is available
from the British Library.

ISBN 978–1–4448–3829–9

Published by
F. A. Thorpe (Publishing)
Anstey, Leicestershire

Set by Words & Graphics Ltd.
Anstey, Leicestershire
Printed and bound in Great Britain by
T. J. International Ltd., Padstow, Cornwall

This book is printed on acid-free paper

COLD CALLING

Fran was fully entitled to park in the disabled bay, a mere hobble from the hospital entrance. She had a stick, after all, not to mention that she was held together by more pins than that dress Elizabeth Hurley had worn to some premiere back in the days when she was still just Hugh Grant's girlfriend.

But something always stopped her. Pride, stubbornness, call it what you will. That useless counsellor her super had wasted public money paying for — 'to help you through your traumatic event' — had gone so far as to suggest that Fran was in denial. As if you could deny the sort of pain that only ever partially disappeared for brief periods at a time and then only when she'd succeeded in taking enough pills and drinking enough whisky to knock herself out.

Some of her able-bodied colleagues parked in the disabled bay anyway. Those

1

who hadn't yet grown tired of visiting Kev, when the prognosis began to suggest that their old mate probably wasn't going to wake up any time soon. And that when he did, he wouldn't be the good old boy they'd all known and loved.

In their minds, their badge gave them the right to ignore petty bureaucracy. They were police, right? But that had never been Fran's style. The law applied just as much to a detective sergeant like herself as it did to any other member of the public.

Beep-beep-beep. The rhythmic beat of the ventilator had been the backing music to her monologue from the moment she'd taken her usual seat next to Kev's bed, round about an hour ago. Fran shifted in her seat. Sometimes she forgot where she was, she relaxed so much when she was here. It was just so peaceful. Nothing on the white walls but public health notices, no furniture apart from the bed and the machinery that was keeping Kev alive. And no sound but the *beep-beep* and her own voice droning on and on.

Poor Kev. He must be sick of the sound

her. Not only that, but he must be kicking himself, locked inside his own little world, for not being able to get a word in edgewise. Of the two of them, he'd always been the talker, and she'd always been the silent one.

'Shut up, Kev. I'm trying to think.'

How often had she said that to him over the years? The only time he was ever silent was when he was shoving a sandwich or a pie in his mouth. Eating helped him think as much as talking — got his thoughts in order, he used to say. So when he wasn't doing one, he had to be doing the other.

A series of images flashed through her mind. The two of them back in the early days, struggling to get to grips with the new computer system. Sitting side by side in the squad car. Then, as they went up the ranks, still side by side, but now each with their own desk.

They'd been side by side the day they'd been sitting in the car waiting for their target. A tip-off had led them to a warehouse on the outskirts of town, down by the river. It was the usual — illegal firearms being unloaded from a boat and transferred into an awaiting lorry.

Should have gone smoothly. All they had to do was wait for backup. But the guys in the Daimler must have got wind that something was up and had driven off at a lick. No use telling Kev to hold his horses. Not when he was at the wheel and pumped for action. He loved all that Sweeney stuff, did Kev.

It all happened so quickly. So unexpectedly. They were gaining on the guys; Kev was a great driver, she'd give him that. Much more confident than she was. He was already ordering the celebratory drinks at the bar when things went dramatically wrong.

'What you having, Fran? Nice glass of Pinot Grigio, is it?'

The last thing she remembered was turning her head towards him to warn him not to count his chickens. Then, *boom!* And *boom* again! Before a black mist descended over her eyes. When she opened them, she was in a hospital bed and Kev was in intensive care. And two months had passed.

The clock on the wall said twenty past seven. Before she visited, she liked to jot down topics of conversation so she wouldn't dry up halfway through the hour. She'd always been the methodical type — ask anyone. Kev would laugh at her and her lists.

'A good police officer listens to his guts,' he used to say. Well, sometimes your guts could let you down.

Glancing down her list for this evening, she realised she'd still not got beyond Topic One: Should I take the new job? Simple enough question, you'd think. And it wasn't as if Kev could say yes or no, after all.

But the more she'd told him about it, the more avenues it led her down. It wasn't just a job, was it, heading up the new cold cases team? It was a solution to a problem. And the problem was her, DS Fran Phoenix, fifty-four years of age, eligible for retirement in a year and, frankly, an embarrassment to the service in which she'd spent the best part of her working life.

'They've been wanting to put me in a

corner ever since I was signed off the sick and pronounced fit for work but unfit for frontline duty.'

Here she was again, going over the same stuff she'd said already. Kev lay there, eyes closed, arms outstretched on the bed, not taking a blind bit of notice.

'They can't get rid of me. They know that. Not till I'm good and ready. So they do the next best thing. Stick me in a job nobody wants.'

Beep-beep.

'And it *is* a corner, too. Down in the basement. No light. No air. A lift! That's all. I'm meant to feel grateful for a lift.'

Beep-beep.

'You wouldn't like it, would you? Stuck behind a desk all day, reading old statements over and over, going back over evidence.'

She sat there waiting, even though there was no reply in the offing. Not now and not any time soon.

'They reckon, if they shove me in the basement, in that corner, with a computer and a phone and three able-bodied officers to run around and do the stuff they think I no longer can, they won't have to look at me. Out of sight, out of mind.'

She took in the still body and the face as pale as the sheets on his bed and the grey stubble around his mouth and chin. His sister would come in and shave him when she visited. Carole was the only other person who came as often as she did herself.

'What would you do, Kev?'

She knew the answer already. He wouldn't sit there like her, full of self-pity and conspiracy theories. Kevin didn't believe in conspiracy theories. 'The only person out to get you is yourself' was one of his sayings. He didn't believe in self-pity either. He loved the police. It had been his life.

Realistically, what was the alternative to turning this job down? She'd have to accept that she wasn't up to it, hand in her badge, take the carriage clock and spend the rest of her life stultifying in the house she'd bought twenty-five years ago but that had never really been her home. Because the police service was her home.

Just like it had always been Kev's.

The door clicked open and a smiling nurse popped her head round the door. 'You still here?' she said as she approached Kev's bed. 'I don't know what you find to talk to him about.'

Fran smiled at the nurse. 'Oh, you know,' she said. 'Life. The universe and everything. And tonight, whether he thinks I should take this new job I've been offered.'

'And what does Kevin say to that?' the nurse asked.

Fran rose to her feet, feeling stiffer than ever after so much time spent seated. 'He thinks I should stop feeling sorry myself and give it a go,' she replied, reaching for her stick.

* * *

Fran had been in her seat for a good fifteen minutes. She wasn't going to risk arriving after everyone else. The last thing she wanted was to witness the awkwardness on the faces of her new team as she, the senior investigating officer, hobbled to her seat at the head of the table, her disability on show for long enough for everyone to ask themselves the question, 'Is she up to it?'

Glancing down at the names on her list, she realised she didn't recognise a single one. Four months was a long time in her job to be out of the loop. One man and three women, if she counted herself. DS Paddy Bradshaw was first on her list. Apparently he'd worked in historical cases before, a quick glance at his potted CV told her, so at least one of them would know what they were doing. Of the two women, the more senior, DC Cheryl Waters, was just back off maternity leave; and the other, Emily Butterworth, was a mere PC with barely two years' service under her belt.

She prayed they'd all arrive together. That way she could get the small talk out of the way in one fell swoop. She suspected they'd be curious to meet her. She'd got used to being a talking point among her contemporaries. People were still swapping theories about the accident even now. It'd go down in history.

Especially if Kev . . .

She wouldn't let her thoughts go there. Not in the daytime time at least. Now, where were the notes for the pep talk she'd decided to start off with? Ah, there they were. Right under her nose.

There was a sudden sharp rap at the door. Fran sat up straight, doing her best to ignore the pain in her hip that this sudden movement had provoked.

'Come in,' she called out.

It was time to make an impression.

* * *

Another week had passed. Once again, Fran found herself sitting by Kevin's bed, bringing him up to date with her news. Once again, there was no change in his condition, apart from the fact that he was wearing different pyjamas tonight and he looked like he'd recently had a shave.

'So. That's my team. A DC, who, when she's not permanently on the phone to her nanny, is showing us photos of Precious Baby Bernice. A PC who looks like she's come to work straight from

10

clubbing, and a right-hand man who clearly thinks his greater experience means *he* should be in charge and not the peg-leg they've put in over him.'

Somewhere in the middle of sounding off about that initial meeting, she discovered she'd taken Kevin's hand in hers. This was happening a lot these days. Funny, because in all the years they'd known each other, they'd never been the touchy-feely type. It was cool to her touch and totally unresponsive to the little squeezes she couldn't help giving it whenever she got irate. But it was *his* hand, and that was something.

Aware she'd slipped into self-pitying mode so soon into her visit, she metaphorically scratched her head for something diverting to tell him. 'Oh, but listen to this, Kev,' she said. 'This morning — you'll laugh — Bradshaw went to put milk in his coffee. And you'll never guess what! He was just about to pour it from this little plastic container when Waters stopped him in the nick of time.'

She paused dramatically for the punch

line. *Beep-beep-beep* went the ventilator. Honestly, its timing was magnificent.

'It was only breast milk she'd expressed in the ladies' half an hour earlier, wasn't it!'

Beep-beep-beep. She hadn't expected a smile. She'd long since stopped expecting anything at all. But it was impossible not to imagine how the old Kev would have reacted. He'd have been dining out on this snippet for days!

She left out the rest of the story. The surprise on Bradshaw's face when Waters launched herself upon him from the other side of the room, followed by the look of shock and disgust on his face when he realised what it was he'd nearly drunk. No sense of humour. No sense of life, even. In fact he wouldn't have been out of place in a bed next to Kevin, wired up to a machine. Not like young Emily, who'd barely been able to keep herself upright, she was laughing that much.

What was the point of filling Kev in on the joke, really? She might as well sit here and read her notes for tomorrow's meeting. Or a magazine, even. It wouldn't make a shred of difference to Kev, after all, would it?

★   ★   ★

'I've labelled this very carefully.'

Cheryl Waters, who moments before had clapped her hands together in order to get everyone's attention, held up the plastic bottle filled with her most recent express delivery of breast milk for everyone else to see, before placing it inside the fridge and taking her seat at the table with everyone else.

Paddy Bradshaw kept his eyes on the papers he was shuffling, distancing himself from any reminder of the events of the previous day. Fran happened to look up and catch young Emily's eye. It was very twinkly, was Emily's gaze.

Fran decided she'd been too hasty in her judgement of the girl. She had a sense of humour, that much was obvious. Plus she had the same issues with Bradshaw that she herself had. Namely that he had the personality of a lump of wood. She could work with this girl.

13

'Happily, I drink mine black,' Fran said, provoking another attack of mirth from Emily. 'Now, to business.'

'I do hope you've taken on board my advice,' Paddy Bradshaw said. 'We do the simple cases first, sign off on them, and straight away it's good news for the crime statistics.'

'You mean the mispers? The poor old souls dredged up from the river or found dead on a park bench in the middle of winter?' said Cheryl. 'I quite agree. With all the advances in forensics, we ought to be able to get a match in no time even if someone's been dead for twenty years or more. Then all we need to do is stick a name up on the website and hope that some relatives come forward.'

Fran looked from one to the other. Amazing how quickly they'd sewn up the order of case precedence between them. Emily's mouth had dropped wide open. She'd be rubbish at poker, that girl. She had one of those faces upon which every emotion was writ large.

'Can't we do all that routine stuff in parallel to the more interesting stuff?' She addressed her question to Fran. This girl, at least, believed in her abilities and hadn't written her off as the token invalid figurehead.

'Easily,' Fran said. 'All that stuff — forensics, websites. It's a job for a wet afternoon. I'm much keener on this new case that MIT have just put our way.'

Suddenly everyone was interested.

'Emma-Jane Maltby, aged six, disappeared from The Priory at Little Ware in the county of Essex somewhere between the evening of Saturday the 19th of August 1989, when she was put to bed by her mother, and the early hours of Sunday the 20th, when her bed was discovered to be empty. The Priory belonged at the time — still does for all we know — to Leonard Rose and his wife Daphne Pointer.' Looking up from her notes, she asked if anyone had ever heard the names before.

'Should we?' Cheryl Waters wanted to know.

'Not necessarily. I was checking to see if I was the only philistine in the team,' Fran said. 'Looks like I'm not. He was a well-known conductor at the time and she was similarly well regarded as a soprano.'

'Classical music and opera?' Emily screwed up her face. 'Not my bag.'

Cheryl pursed her lips in disapproval. 'Can we get on with this, please?' she asked.

'Sure.'

Fran pressed on. During that weekend, there had been a number of people present. The Roses, naturally, and their three grown-up daughters. The younger daughter, Carola, had invited a boyfriend who turned up late that evening. The middle daughter, Lorelei, turned up alone. Emma-Jane came with her mother, Aften, the oldest of the Rose daughters, and Joshua Maltby, her husband and Emma-Jane's father.

'I think I remember something about this case,' Paddy Bradshaw, who'd been listening intently while scribbling notes at the same time, piped up.

'Perhaps you'd care to share,' said Fran.

He cleared his throat and put a hand to his tie to straighten it. 'Well, to be honest,

I can't remember the details,' he said.

Fran beamed at him. 'Well, it was twenty-five years ago, after all,' she said generously.

Just as she'd expected. He didn't know a damn thing about the case.

'I wasn't even born then,' said Emily.

Cheryl Waters shot her a look of pure venom. She couldn't have been more than thirty-two herself, Fran thought, so why she was wasting her energy being jealous of a kid who was still wet behind the ears, she didn't know. Unless she just wanted Fran to get on with it.

'Also present on that weekend were Betty Taverner the housekeeper, and her partner Tony Best, who did odd jobs around the house and grounds.'

'Lots of suspects, then,' Emily said.

'True,' said Fran. 'However, no body has ever been found.' She waited a moment for this to sink in.

'So why do the major incident team want us to look into it just at this particular moment in time?' Paddy Bradshaw wanted to know.

Fran reached for the glass of water at

17

her elbow. She was in dire need of one of her painkillers, but no way would she demean herself by taking a pill in front of an audience, two-thirds of which had already written her off.

She took a few sips, pondering how to answer. The thing was, this was nothing to do with MIT. She was instigating this enquiry herself. Twenty-five years ago she'd been a newly qualified PC. She'd met Kev on this case. He was newly qualified too, as a detective constable. The whole team had worked hard; really pulled together.

They hadn't solved the crime. But she and Kev had become friends. When the case had been closed — or rather, put into cold storage — he'd persuaded her to make the sideways move into CID because if they'd have him, then they'd definitely have her too, he said.

The case had been taken off the shelf and dusted off twice since. But both times a blank had been drawn. Other enquiries had failed just like the first. She'd never forgotten it though, never quite been able to shake it off. And she

18

knew Kev felt just the same.

'I'd die happy,' he'd told her, less than a year ago when they'd both had one too many at some celebration or other and found themselves discussing it once more, 'if I could get closure on the disappearance of that little girl.'

She was doing this for Kev.

* * *

'Why *this* case, Fran?' the super wanted to know. He sat at his desk, imposing in his dress uniform. Looked like he had something important planned for later, Fran thought.

It was a relief to finally arrive at the topic Fran really wanted to discuss. The super's insistence on a blow-by-blow account on Kev's progress had gone on long enough, and by this time the urge to remind him of the visiting hours at the general so he could go and see for himself had become almost overwhelming.

The case had been revisited a couple of times already, as well she knew, he reminded her. They'd gone over the area

19

around The Priory again and taken in and re-questioned suspects, but nothing had come out of any of it. And without a body, no amount of new forensic discoveries could help uncover a murderer.

'I know all that, sir,' Fran said. 'But this time it'll be different.'

'How so?'

'Because the last two times were pretty half-hearted attempts,' she said. 'Not all the locals who could have seen something the weekend Emma-Jane went missing from her room were re-interviewed. Details were never followed up, phone calls never returned.'

The super furrowed his brow.

'There's no criticism implied, sir,' she reassured him. 'We were overstretched both times we went back, is all. I've checked, and we had several other major incidents running parallel to both the subsequent Maltby reinvestigations. Hardly surprising we were short on manpower.'

'True. True.'

'But it'll be different now we've

established a dedicated team of investigators.'

'I admire your optimism, Fran,' he said. 'It's inspiring to see just how quickly you've bounced back to your old self.'

Fran recognized flannel when she heard it. Bounced back. That was a good one. What he really wanted was for her to bounce right out of the force and out of his life so he wouldn't keep being reminded of the eye-watering amount of compo her union were claiming for her and Kev.

'There's something else too, sir,' she said. 'What's today's date?'

The super's desk calendar showed 17/08/2015. It was Monday. 'See for yourself,' he said, waving his arm in its direction.

'Don't you see? It's practically twenty-five years to the week that the little girl disappeared. On the last two occasions, when some effort was made to revisit the case, one was in spring — April '95 — and the other in autumn, October '06.'

'I don't quite see . . . '

'Think about it,' she said. 'People's

21

memories of a significant event are often triggered when something reminds them of that event. If just *one* of the sights or sounds or scents of August 2015 in the Essex countryside evokes some memory of August 1989 in any one of the residents of Little Ware or its surroundings, then who knows what it might lead to?'

The super glanced at the clock on the wall and checked it against his own timepiece. Finally he spoke. 'Very well,' he said. 'I can see how keen you are.'

And I can see just how much more important than this meeting with me is the next thing on your to-do list is, Fran thought, triumphant nevertheless.

'Though you mustn't overtax yourself,' he said as he opened the door to let her out, a gallant gesture he'd never made before in all the years he'd been her boss.

'Don't worry, sir. If I do, I won't be asking the union to put in another claim.'

He had the grace to blush.

★　★　★

Fran had been nervous about relinquishing control of a car to someone else since the accident. But without a doubt she'd made the right decision, choosing the youngest member of the team to accompany her on this overnight trip.

Emily Butterworth was a good driver. She kept both hands firmly on the wheel and her eyes on the road at all times; and unlike Kev, she didn't seem to feel the urge to hurl expletives at those other drivers who had the audacity to share the Queen's Highway with her.

Right now the two of them were on the motorway, heading for The Priory at Little Ware. Yesterday evening, just before she'd left work for the day and gone home to relieve the nanny of the care of Precious Bernice, Cheryl Waters had passed over the information that although The Priory had changed hands since 1989, it remained within the family and was now the permanent home of the middle Rose daughter, Lorelei.

To add to this piece of good luck, the housekeeper Betty Taverner hadn't moved from her cottage at the end of the terrace, either. It was this information that cemented Fran's decision to head for Little Ware the very next day. That and the fact that the weather forecast was brilliant, and if she had to spend another day in that damn basement she'd go mad.

'Ring ahead and tell them I'm coming,' she'd ordered Cheryl. 'And while you're on the phone, you might think about booking two single rooms at the nearest hotel. I'm going to need a fellow officer.'

'Oh, I couldn't possibly accompany you, ma'am,' Cheryl had replied. 'I'm still breastfeeding.'

Choosing Cheryl Waters as a travelling companion had never even occurred to Fran. The situation could have become awkward; but by employing the kind of fast thinking Kev used to compliment her on, she managed to convince Cheryl that though her presence would be a great loss, it was an excellent opportunity to give Emily a bit of experience. By the end of it, you'd almost think she'd done the DC a favour.

It was a hot afternoon when they set out. *Simpsons* clouds skittered across the sky in a madcap race with the birds, trees acknowledged them with a rustle of leaves as the car sped by, and the windscreen was an armageddon of slaughtered flies.

August, in all its splendour, thought Fran, appreciating nature through the window before returning her gaze to the rather scruffy file on her lap. It contained every statement that had ever been obtained pertaining to the Maltby case. And since the case had been revisited twice, it had to be said that the file was on the heavy side.

Had the super been right this morning, when he'd implied that she'd bitten off more than she could chew? Very probably. But she'd promised Kev she was going to crack this one, and she had no intention of breaking her promise.

Emily's voice broke into her thoughts. 'Isn't Google brilliant?' she said in her warm Leeds accent.

Fran stopped her sifting and glanced at her companion. 'How do you mean?'

'Well, you know. One click and I can find out all I need to know about what happened in any year in the UK. Since records began, of course.'

Fran wondered where all this was leading.

'Did you know, for instance, that in 1989 Sky TV launched its satellite service over here? Or that this was the year of the Hillsborough disaster as well as the year electronic tagging was introduced?'

'Oh, research.' Fran was impressed. 'Good girl!'

Blushing obviously came easily to red-haired Emily, whose pretty round face was splashed with freckles.

'What else happened?' Fran wanted to know.

'Lots of things. Bob Geldof did 'Do They Know It's Christmas' for the first time. The General Assembly of the Church of England voted for the ordination of women. Oh, and Margaret Thatcher had a grandson.'

'Oh, I remember that. 'We have become a grandmother.'' Fran chuckled.

'Pardon?' Emily said without taking her eyes off the road.

'She said it when she came out of Number 10 to make the announcement.

That's when it became obvious even to those who hadn't noticed it before that power had gone to her head.'

'You didn't like her then?'

'I don't like any of them.'

'Me neither. Sooner or later they all overreach themselves, don't they, them in charge?'

She was quite a philosopher, was little Emily, for all her twenty-two years, Fran decided.

'What do you remember about 1989?' Another blush. 'Oh, sorry. I'm being nosy. You'll probably want to ignore that question.'

Fran chuckled. She wasn't the slightest bit offended, she said, already casting her mind back to the year in question. 1989. It was a lifetime ago. She was nineteen years of age, still wet behind the ears. 'I was younger than you,' she said dreamily. 'This was my first case, you know — the disappearance of Emma-Jane Maltby.'

'No way!' Emily gripped the steering wheel more tightly, but her gaze never faltered from the road ahead.

'I met my old buddy Kev on that case too. He was a few years older than me. A newly qualified detective constable.' She smiled to herself. 'Thought he knew everything back then. Turned out he knew nothing.'

At the mention of Kevin, the atmosphere grew heavy.

'Is he . . . ?' Emily's voice dropped to a murmur. 'Is he going to come out of his coma?' she said.

'He'd flaming well better had,' Fran replied. It was all she could do to control the quiver in her voice. Every, every time she thought about him, something went badly wrong with her insides. Just then she thought she spotted the turn off to Little Ware. It couldn't have come at a more convenient time. Thankfully, Emily had spotted it too.

'Nearly there,' she said, indicating left. 'Pretty round here, isn't it?'

Discreet too, Fran thought. They were going to get on very well.

★ ★ ★

The Priory had changed very little in the twenty-five years since Fran had last visited it, at least outwardly; its air of faded eccentricity and charm remaining solidly intact. Quite how old the building was, she had no idea. At least a couple of hundred years, no doubt. She remembered being told that the terrace of four cottages had once been farm labourers' dwellings.

All four cottages had come up for sale towards the end of the 1940s as the labourers gradually deserted the land for the towns and cities after the war. The Roses — Leonard Rose and his first wife — snapped up three of the cottages, knocking down walls and turning them into one dwelling. They'd fallen in love with the idea of a retreat far away from their London world of concerts and smart dinners. And it was a draw for their friends too, all of whom were particularly fascinated by the idea of having a graveyard and a church with a spire in one's back yard.

Some twenty years later, after the first Mrs Rose had died, Leonard Rose and his second wife rescued the tiny school-house on the furthest edge of their land, when due to the declining population, it came under threat of demolition.

Unfortunately, Emily had turned off the main road rather too quickly, due in no small part to Fran's eagerness to divert the conversation away from Kev. It soon became clear that they'd taken the back road by mistake, where they'd been forced to abandon the car ten minutes' walk away from The Priory, due to the great big hole that threatened to swallow them if they attempted to proceed any further.

It had been a struggle for Fran to complete the rest of the journey on foot, but determination got her there. To give her credit, Emily steadfastly chose to ignore Fran's difficulties. Presumably she'd already worked out that Fran was feeling sensitive and didn't want to exacerbate her mood by treating her like an invalid.

The only thing she had done, to lighten Fran's burden was to relieve her of the bulky file she'd been holding onto all the way here. Now she was skimming one of the pages she'd removed and giving it her full concentration while Fran stood leaning on her stick, getting her breath back and taking in the view.

'So it's the middle daughter, Lorelei Rose, who owns The Priory now,' Emily said.

Fran decided it was safe to risk a reply, now she'd pretty much got both her breath and her composure back. 'That's right. At the time of Emma-Jane's disappearance, she would have been in her late twenties.'

'According to her statement, she arrived Friday late afternoon. The older Roses, Leonard and Daphne and Carola — she's the youngest daughter — had already arrived. Shall I just remind you who else was there?'

Fran nodded. She'd read it all before. But it was hot and she was tired and her painkillers were wearing off. One more time could only help. Then they'd go inside, and hopefully Lorelei Rose would offer them a seat and a desperately needed cup of tea. She should have been expecting them, after all.

'The Maltbys — Aften, the oldest Rose daughter, her husband Joshua, and little Emma-Jane — arrived at five-thirty. Carola had gone straight out again, on arrival at the cottage, to say hi to Betty at the end cottage. And to see if Betty's daughter, Beth was around — they were good friends, apparently.'

Fran allowed her gaze to wander round the garden. It really hadn't changed a jot. From this spot, she could just about see the huge trampoline she remembered gazing longingly at more than once, when she'd been ordered to stand on guard down by the schoolhouse, to keep the rubberneckers at bay.

'When she came back, she told Emma-Jane she'd been playing with Betty's new kittens; and as soon as Emma-Jane heard that, she demanded to be allowed to go and see them too,' Emily's words broke into her thoughts. 'There was a row, apparently, according to Lorelei. Between Aften and her husband. *She* didn't want Emma-Jane dashing off when she'd only just got here, and *he* didn't see the point of being in the country if kids couldn't roam freely.' She raised her head and met Fran's gaze. 'I bet he came to regret saying that,' she added.

Fran nodded. 'You could be right,' she said. She'd been half-aware for some time now that the two of them were being watched. Emily had noticed it too.

'There's someone been staring at us from the upstairs window of the end cottage for the last five minutes,' she said.

Fran followed her gaze, but whoever it was had gone.

'A woman,' Emily went on. 'White-haired. Sort of bent over. Cross-looking. Would it be Betty Taverner?'

Fran caught herself just in time saying it couldn't possibly be Betty, not from that description. But then she remembered that twenty-five years had passed. Who'd have thought all those years ago, when she'd been guarding the entrance to the Rose's land and desperately fancying a turn on the trampoline while also feeling ashamed of herself for having such wicked thoughts when a six-year-old child had gone missing, that she'd be standing here leaning on a stick for support? Right now the chances of her being able to get up on that trampoline, let alone actually use it, were about as slim as her chances of running the London Marathon.

'Well, whoever she is, she's gone now,' Emily said.

'Except as one door closes, another . . . '

' . . . bursts open. Oh my!'

Emily had barely finished her alternative ending to the well-known proverb when a tall nut-brown woman in shorts and a thin strappy T-shirt came hurtling towards them, waving her arms frantically. If she'd had dogs, Fran thought, she would have set them loose by now.

'I can't believe you have the nerve to turn up like this, raking over old ground!' The woman spoke so fast she almost swallowed her words.

Fran stepped forward and held out her hand in the vain hope her antagonist would consider shaking it. 'Detective Sergeant Fran Phoenix,' she said. 'And this is PC Emily Butterworth.'

'I don't care who you are! I don't want you here. My sister told that other police officer the same.'

The woman was growing more agitated by the minute. The afternoon had grown hotter, and in the humidity the woman's expensively coiffured and tinted hair was fast losing its bounce.

'Don't you think we've suffered enough, my husband and I and the rest of our family, with you lot coming back here as regular as clockwork with as little idea of what you're doing each time you come as you did the first time?'

'Aften! Darling! Come back inside. Please!'

Fran had been concentrating so hard trying to work out the identity of their initial assailant — she'd already settled on it being Aften even before the second woman of a similar age and build came running out of the cottage and tipped them off — that she failed to hear the crunching of the gravel behind her. It looked like not only Lorelei but Betty Taverner had decided to join the fray.

'You heard her! Beggar off! Leave this

family alone!' she snapped.

They were getting it from all sides.

'Please, ladies!' Fran summoned all the authority she could muster. She addressed her words to Aften Maltby, who appeared to have run out of steam, finally. Her sister had joined her and was now comforting her, one arm around her shoulder, as a deflated Aften leaned into her.

'It's not our intention to cause you or your family any stress, Mrs Maltby. If we could just come inside and have a little chat.'

The sun beat down vociferously upon the small group. It was surely this fact, Fran decided, rather than any thoughts of hospitality on Lorelei Rose's part that finally gained them entrance into the cottage.

Once inside the temperature may have been cooler but the atmosphere seethed and bubbled. A silent Lorelei busied herself making tea, while Aften sat herself down at the table, refusing to meet anyone's eye.

Betty Taverner, on the contrary, followed every single movement Fran made with a suspicious gaze. As for Emily, when her phone rang she shot out of the door like a greyhound from a trap, obviously delighted at the prospect of a reprieve.

She was back almost immediately. Looking grave she signaled to Fran to come outside. Excusing herself she made her way outside, to where Emily had found some shade beneath an old gnarled tree.

'That was Cheryl on the phone,' she said.

'Oh yes?'

Right now Fran wasn't feeling all that well disposed towards DS Cheryl Waters. Couldn't she have mentioned that the reception they'd hoped for was not the one they ought to expect? Forewarned being forearmed and all that.

'It's about Tony Best.'

'Who? Remind me.'

'Betty's partner. As was. He was living with her at the time of Emma-Jane's disappearance.'

'What about him?' Fran said.

'She — Cheryl — looked him up. He's

in poor health. Been living with his daughter, but he gets a bit much for her from time to time. Right now he's in respite. And this is the interesting bit.'

She paused to take a breath and consult her notes.

'Cheryl paid a visit to the place he's staying. She has an old aunt living there, so she thought she'd kill two birds with one stone and look in on the way home last night. And she received some extremely interesting information from one of carers there,' she went on.

'What sort of information?'

'According to this carer, Tony Best, who hasn't been in the best of health this past couple of weeks, has been shouting in his sleep.'

'Shouting what?' Fran asked.

'Emma-Jane's name. Waking up in a cold sweat. Crying. Crazy-eyed. Like a man with something terrible on his conscience.' She eyed Fran warily. 'What do you think, Fran? Do we have a suspect?'

★ ★ ★

Afternoon tea at The Greyhound, where Fran and Emily checked in round about an hour later, was an infinitely more convivial affair than it would have been back at The Priory, what with Betty Taverner channelling Mrs Danvers and Aften Maltby blanking them entirely.

'Tuck in,' Fran said.

Emily's eyes were as round as saucers. 'It's like the Ritz, isn't it?' She helped herself to a dainty triangle of a smoked-salmon sandwich. 'Not that I've been. But, you know, as you'd imagine it.'

Fran poured the tea. Since the accident, she'd found it difficult to get as interested in food as she once was. But she could see that by the time they'd found their hotel, after being ejected from Lorelei Rose's kitchen even before the kettle had boiled on the ancient Aga, poor Emily was almost fainting from hunger.

When she'd spied a waitress sallying forth from the kitchen bearing an impressive cake stand crammed with a variety of delicious goodies, all jostling for space, she needed no further encouragement than Emily's expression of longing to place an order for the same. The treat would have to come out of her own pocket, since their expenses wouldn't cover it. But she didn't mind that. Emily deserved it after all that driving in such gruelling heat. And the rest in this comfortable chair, a cushion at her back and plenty of space to stretch out her leg, was already working its magic on her too, after so long in the car.

Not to mention the fact that slowly, slowly, with each sip of her tea, she felt her blood pressure returning to normal and she no longer felt like strangling Cheryl Waters, though she knew that if she got on the phone to her too soon she'd probably explode. *Just wait another fifteen minutes*, she told herself. *You'll be even calmer.* But no, it was no use. Beggar the blood pressure. She couldn't restrain herself a second longer.

'You carry on, Emily,' she said as she struggled to her feet. 'Just save me a couple of those little macaroons. I need to pay a visit to the little girls' room.'

Once there, Fran whipped out her phone and punched in Cheryl's name.

Cheryl answered immediately, her voice breathy and excited.

'Ah, Fran. Excellent,' she said. 'You'll be ringing about Tony Best. Now, I've spoken to the carer. But Best was out of sorts, and I was informed I couldn't interview him just yet. I guess I'll have to wait for a call before I get the go-ahead.'

'Why didn't you inform me that Lorelei Rose specifically said she didn't want to speak to the police before I dragged ourselves all the way here?'

From the long silence that followed, this *wasn't* the response Cheryl was expecting. But Fran wouldn't have reacted to her opening words so brusquely if Cheryl hadn't spoken to her as if *she* were the DS and not Fran.

'I — I don't think she did,' said Cheryl. 'Did she?' she added feebly.

'Absolutely she did. Not only did she specify that to you, but when she discovered we were coming anyway, she called her sister and her neighbour in the end cottage for backup.'

'Well maybe she did, then. But I didn't think it was important to tell you as long as I gave them the message.'

If that wasn't an admission of guilt, Fran didn't know what was. 'Of course it was important!' she said. 'If I'd known she didn't want us to come down, I'd have got on the phone and done my best to talk her round. We can't afford not to have Emma-Jane Maltby's mother on our side, Cheryl. They've been through enough. Now they think their world is about to be turned upside down one more time.'

'I can only apologise again,' Cheryl said.

Fran resisted pointing out that actually this was the first time.

'I was just trying to protect you from any unnecessary stress.' Cheryl's tone was abject now. 'I didn't think you needed to know the details.'

Fran clenched her fist. If she'd had something to punch, then she would have punch it. But all there was in front of her was the mirror. And she didn't fancy stitches on top of all her other injuries.

'First of all, DC Waring, I do not need protecting. I am your senior officer, and as such I am well able to protect myself. Secondly, details are my business. Never try to keep them hidden from me if you want to stay on my team.' Saying that gave her a great deal of satisfaction.

'I'll make sure it doesn't happen again.'

'Good. Now, I'm heading back to my room and my computer. I'd be grateful if you could forward me the statement from Tony Best's carer and the name and number of the manager of the care home.'

'So you don't want me to interview Best, then?'

'No, I don't think I do, actually,' she said. 'I think I'd prefer it if you left Tony Best to me.'

With that she rang off, and washed her hands very thoroughly with the deliciously scented liquid soap provided before slathering them with the equally fragrant lotion.

★　★　★

On Fran's return, Emily jumped up to greet her like an overenthusiastic puppy. 'So, what did Carol say? Has she interviewed him yet?'

Fran explained that Tony Best was having an off day, so until they heard back from the manager of the care home, the best thing would be to put their minds to something else. 'And it'll be me interviewing him, not Cheryl,' she added, helping herself to a macaroon. 'I just hope whatever it is he's been yelling in his sleep is actually relevant and not just the ravings of an old man.'

Emily agreed.

'So in the time we have left today, we need to prepare for the interview. I'd like you to read through Best's statements and find out what people say about him. How much did he have to do with the Rose family and the Maltbys? Everything is relevant.'

Emily rubbed her hands together gleefully. She was going to enjoy this, she said. Soon after, once they'd demolished the contents of the cake stand and emptied the teapot, the two women parted ways, each to her own room.

Now Fran sat at her desk and scrolled

through her laptop. She should have been thinking about her case, but she felt too heavy and sleepy with cake to concentrate. Unsurprisingly, her thoughts turned to Kev. Would he miss her tonight when she failed to turn up to visit him? Or was that just too fanciful an idea?

Maybe she should ring the hospital and check with the nurse on duty. She'd been there so often she knew them all by name now — Martina, Duncan, Shirelle and Mary, the four guardian angels who kept watch over Kev twenty-four/seven. Well, if she couldn't be there herself, at least she could rest assured that he'd be in safe hands.

Just then, her phone bleeped. It was the super. He sounded agitated. And whenever he was agitated, he had a tendency to cut straight to the chase.

'The Emily-Rose case,' he said. 'You're to cancel your hotel room right away and return home.'

'Why's that, sir?'

If Fran was about to get a pep talk about squandering the taxpayers' money on expensive hotels, she might as well listen to it with one eye on her emails, she decided.

And here was a very interesting one — forwarded just three minutes ago from Cheryl from one Susan Jones, manager of Fairfax Rise, the old people's home where Tony Best was resident. Mr Best seemed much better, and she would be happy to receive Detective Sergeant Phoenix at the home in the morning so that she could conduct her interview with him.

'We've had a complaint from Lorelei Rose.'

Fran's heart sank.

'Apparently you turned up at her cottage this afternoon causing great distress to her sister, the mother of the little girl who went missing. So much distress, in fact, that the lady in question had a severe asthma attack and the doctor had to be called.'

'I'm very sorry to hear that,' Fran said. 'It wasn't our intention to cause distress to anyone.'

She could have landed Cheryl in it at this point, but that wasn't her way.

46

Besides, she'd laid that particular problem to rest. And it would be much more exciting to have a ding-dong with the super. What did he mean, abandon the case and come home, just when things were getting interesting?

'With respect, sir, the case of the missing girl remains unsolved,' she said. 'To pull us out now might turn out to be a bad decision, and one you might come to regret.'

The silence at the other end of the line suggested the super was considering this deeply. His fear of being torn apart by the press was legendary.

'Because?'

'Because we have a lead.' Briefly but succinctly, she filled him about the Tony Best situation.

'Hmm. I see,' he said when he'd heard her out. He thought for a moment. 'Can you go and interview him now?'

Fran didn't think so. It was getting late, and bedtime at Fairfax Rise was probably already imminent. The super conceded she was probably right. Better leave it till the morning when Best would be fresh.

'But before then, you must promise me not to do anything else to agitate the family, okay?' he said.

'You have my word, sir.'

And she meant it — for now. But if there was even just one whiff of anything untoward in any of the statements Emily was currently going through, then she'd be onto them right away.

* * *

'Are you sure about this?'

Emily had brought them down the right road to Little Ware this morning. She'd parked the car expertly alongside a battered old jeep they both imagined must belong to Betty Taverner. The gleaming BMW opposite was surely out of her league and probably belonged to one of the Rose sisters, they agreed.

'He doesn't want any more trouble with Emma-Jane's mother,' Fran said reassuringly. 'We're not visiting Emma-Jane's mother, are we? We're just having a word with Betty about her ex, en route to interviewing him. We don't want to get to the nursing home too early; and anyway, it's not as if Tony Best is going anywhere, is it?'

'I suppose not,' Emily said, reaching for her cap and setting it on her head, resigned to whatever the fates were about to throw at her.

'Cheer up,' Fran said. 'If anybody's head is going to be on the block for this at all, it won't be yours. You're just obeying orders.'

'Now, where have I heard that before?' Emily opened the door with a sigh and stepped lightly out into the still cool morning air.

It took Fran a great deal longer to get out her side, but she managed in the end. Just like the previous day, they both felt they were being watched.

'Upstairs window again,' Emily said. 'It's as if she has her own personal radar system.'

'And now here she comes.' Fran took a step forward and extended her hand in greeting as moments later Betty Taverner appeared at her front door, wiping her hands on her apron, before striding towards them.

'You lot have got a damn cheek!'

The look she gave Fran's extended hand was a withering one. Deciding she'd had enough of humouring the woman, Fran withdrew it and settled on another strategy. 'I can see you're straight-talking woman, Mrs Taverner,' she said. 'Well, that suits me fine, because so am I. I want to talk to you about your ex-partner, Tony Best.'

The mention of him obviously unsettled her. She was immediately on her guard. 'You'd best come inside,' she said. 'I think I left the kettle on.'

The interior of the cottage had a gloomy feel about it, thanks to the tiny windows that let in little light, even on such a bright morning as this. With three of them in the tiny kitchen that was crammed with far too much furniture, all of it dark and heavy, it felt overcrowded too.

Betty Taverner gestured to the kitchen table, where Fran found a stool and perched upon it with some difficulty; while Emily, tall and sturdy at five eight, hovered behind her, trying to make herself smaller.

'What do you want with Tony, anyway? I ain't seen him in years.' She removed the whistling kettle from the hob but made no attempt to make tea with its contents.

'But he did once live with you here as your partner, didn't he?'

'We were man and wife in all but name.'

'You had a daughter together too, didn't you? Beth, wasn't it?'

Betty nodded. Her expression had become wary.

'I'm assuming she was Tony's daughter?'

Another nod.

'Does she live locally?'

'I couldn't tell you where she's living at the moment,' Betty said. 'My daughter and I no longer keep in touch.'

'I'm sorry to hear that, Betty. It's sad when families break up.'

Betty shrugged. 'That depends. My daughter and I never saw eye to eye from her being very young. Sometimes it's best just to cut the ties.'

Fran could imagine most young girls with spirit would hate being stuck in this poky cottage in the sticks. Was it this that had made Beth Taverner restless? Very likely, Fran thought. No doubt it made her desire to escape even stronger on those occasions that her friend, the young Carola Rose, came down occasionally for weekends and Christmases and the like, reminding her of the big wide world that existed beyond the boundaries of this tiny hamlet.

'At the time of Emma-Jane's disappearance, Beth wasn't here, I believe.'

'That's right. She had a job in Colchester. One of the big hotels.'

'But Tony Best was here, wasn't he?'

'He didn't have nothing to do with that little girl's disappearance!'

'You seem very sure about that, Betty,' Fran said.

'He wouldn't harm a fly,' Betty replied. 'And if you knew this case as much as you think you do, then you'd know he'd been taken in and questioned and completely exonerated.'

'Did you know he's currently staying at Fairfax Rise, a residential home on the other side of Colchester?'

'I didn't, no.' The news had obviously come as a shock. 'We lost touch years ago. Last I heard, he'd set up home with a barmaid Long Melford way.'

It occurred to Fran that Betty Taverner kept an extremely tenuous grasp on her relationships. 'Respite care, apparently,' Fran continued. 'To give his daughter — his *other* daughter, that is, a bit of a break from looking after him.'

If it hurt her to think of her ex being cared for by a daughter she knew nothing about, when she herself wasn't even on speaking terms with her own, she didn't show it.

'Apparently he's been saying things in his sleep,' Fran said.

Betty's dark eyes darted around the room before finally landing back on Fran. 'What sort of things?'

Fran shrugged. 'Well, that's what we intend to find out. We're on our way to see him now, actually.'

'I could make you a cup of tea.'

The sudden change in Betty Taverner's manner from guarded to conciliatory was as weird as it was unexpected. 'That's very kind, Betty, but we really ought to be getting a move on,' she said. Fran rose from her seat with as much grace as her sore hip would allow. Turning to Emily, she asked her if she had any questions for Betty.

'As a matter of fact, I do,' she said. 'You must have been devastated when Emma-Jane went missing. According to several statements given by various members of the Rose family, the little girl was in and out of your cottage like it was her own, whenever she came down with her family.'

'Yes, that's right. And that's why there was all this talk of Tony being implicated somehow. But he never took her or did her any harm. And if you ask me, the reason he's ranting in his sleep will be because he's reliving those dreadful interrogations your lot put him through.'

The room fell silent apart from the fractured sound of Betty getting her breath back after her tirade. Fran threw

Emily a glance that said it really was time to go.

'I never actually got to ask her my question,' Emily said as they walked the short distance to the car.

Fran laughed. 'What was it?'

'Well,' she said, 'I don't actually need to ask it. I can call it in. But it's about the BMW.'

'What about it?'

'Didn't you see the log book on the sideboard? And the keys hanging off the hook? Very flashy logos Beamers have on everything. My uncle has one, which is how I recognised it.'

Fran shook her head. She hadn't noticed either, she said.

'Well, my question was simply, did the Beamer outside belong to her? Because if it did, well, how did she get the money to buy it?'

'That's actually two questions,' Fran said. 'And they're both good ones. I'll call it in en route to the care home.'

If something smells odd, then it probably is. How many times had she heard Kev say that in all the years they'd worked together? The fact that Betty Taverner owned a brand-new BMW might mean something or it might mean nothing at all.

'Maybe we should talk to Carola Rose as a priority,' Fran said once they were on the road. 'Betty's cottage was her first port of call on the weekend Emma-Jane went missing. She and Beth Taverner were obviously great friends. Might be worth checking if they still keep in touch.'

'I managed to find an address for her,' Emily said. 'Though I can't swear it's up to date. We could take a bit of a detour and call in on the off chance she's at home. According to my information, she doesn't live too far from Fairfax Rise. Be interesting to hear what she has to say about the rift between Betty and her.'

'Not to mention her instincts about Best,' Fran added. 'Now, let me put that call in to traffic.'

It was a matter of moments to discover that Betty Taverner was indeed the owner of the BMW. Fran gave Emily the thumbs-up. As soon as she put down the phone, it began ringing again. It was Cheryl. She sounded chastened and tentative.

'This might be something and it might be nothing,' she said. 'You need to decide.'

Good. So Cheryl had finally realised who was in charge of the case.

'You've always said there's bound to be a backlog of unfollowed-up leads with this case,' Cheryl went on. 'Well, you were right.'

Fran held her breath.

'I thought I'd ring a few numbers. Most of them are unobtainable now. But there was this one woman I rang. Local. Went off on her gap year, apparently, just after the Maltby girl went missing, so didn't find out about the case till she returned home ten months later.'

'Go on.'

'When she eventually did hear about it, she rang in to report something she thought might have been relevant. But nobody got back to her even though she thinks she may have called back a couple more times. Naturally she let it lie after that, went off to uni and got on with her life.'

'And if you'd not checked in with her this morning, she'd still be letting it lie. Great work, Cheryl!' She owed her that.

'Her name's Deborah Butcher,' Cheryl said, acknowledging the compliment with the smile in her voice. 'She lives in Freckleford. Three miles outside Little Ware. Can you get over there if I give you the address?'

'Give it me now,' Fran said, 'and I'll punch it into the satnav. We're on our way.'

★   ★   ★

Deborah Butcher, clad in paint-stained overalls colourfully accessorized with paint-splashed face and hands, blinked at them from behind rimless glasses. Her frizzy mane of dark brown hair was pulled back from her face and tied with a scarf, perhaps in an attempt to protect at least this one small fraction of her person from coming under further paint attack. She was just in the middle of something, she said, or she would have cleaned herself up.

Fran hated to be the one to drag Deborah away from her muse. But she and Emily had another two visits to make after this one and time was of the essence, particularly as far as Tony Best, who wasn't in the best of health, was concerned.

Deborah led them through into the small council house and up the uncarpeted stairs to the largest bedroom; or, as she described it, *my studio*. Much better to talk in there, she explained, since the rest of the house was a bit of a mess. Fran was well qualified to vouch for that, having caught a glimpse of the pile of washing-up in the kitchen through the open door.

Everywhere she looked, hanging on walls and propped up against walls were canvases, some finished, some blank. Fran guessed — correctly it turned out — that Deborah, a woman in her early forties now, lived alone. It would take an extremely tolerant partner to put up with that amount of clutter.

Her degree had been in fine art, she explained — which was a pretty useless one for anyone wanting to make a decent living, as her parents were always reminding her. Fortunately, money had never interested her that much, she said. And anyway, if they'd wanted her to become a banker or a big-shot lawyer, they shouldn't have set up home in the heart of Constable country, just a few miles from where the artist had painted his famous *Haywain*. Living here, how could she have escaped falling in love with the idea of becoming an artist herself?

Not that Deborah Butcher and Constable would have had much in common, stylistically. Her canvases were covered in nudes — male and female — and none of them particularly attractive, either, from what Fran could see. *Great big slabs of meat* was how Emily would describe them later, when they were well away from the house. For now, she simply glanced at them suspiciously before quickly averting her eyes.

Deborah cleared a space for the two

women on an old squashed sofa hidden beneath a badly stained throw. Unfortunately, the space was immediately snatched from beneath them by a fiery orange cat that challenged its harassed mistress with an icy stare to do something about moving him, if she dared. She apologised profusely on the cat's behalf. 'I live with a tyrant,' she said.

'Never mind,' Fran said, breezily. 'Possession is nine tenths of the law, after all.'

Tomorrow she had an appointment with a chiropractor recommended to her by one of the specials, Mags, who swore that if anyone could sort Fran out, then this one could. She was an absolute witch, apparently, who in another age would very likely have been burnt at the stake for her magic powers.

Tomorrow couldn't come fast enough for Fran. Meanwhile, she was going to have to rely on willpower and ibuprofen. She'd give Deborah Butcher ten minutes, that was all, then it was back in the car where she'd be able to sit down and top up her pain relief.

'Right, so what is it you think you saw on the night of the 19th of August 1989, Deborah?' she said.

'Did they tell you I'd made a few attempts to report what I thought I'd seen as soon as I came back from my gap year?'

Fran nodded.

'I just assumed that they didn't think what I had to say was relevant. Of course, it still might not be. In which case, I'm sorry if I'm wasting your time.'

'Just tell us, Deborah, and let us judge whether it's relevant or not.'

Deborah, squatting on a stool at the foot of her easel, began her story. She remembered the night clearly, she said, because it was the day she'd turned eighteen. She'd arranged a bit of party at the local pub, The Hole in the Wall.

'It was a bit of a dump — still is — but it was a pub and we could get alcohol, and that was the main thing. And since the buses are so infrequent round these parts and none of us had transport of our own, it was really our

62

only choice for a night out.'

Her parents had coughed up for a room off the main bar, and there'd been food too. Of course they'd all had far too much to drink, being the age they were, and Deborah had gone outside for some fresh air because she thought she might be sick if she didn't.

'Too much information, I know,' she said apologetically.

'Don't worry, we've heard worse,' Emily said.

Deborah tilted her head to one side and scrutinised Emily for a long time. 'You know, you have a real look of Lizzie Siddal about you,' she said. 'That coppery hair, your height, the long neck.'

'Who's Lizzie Siddal?' Emily wanted to know.

Deborah Butcher opened her mouth like someone about to launch into a lecture. Fran gave an inward sigh. Ten minutes? It would be half an hour at this rate. Any minute now, Deborah would be asking poor Emily to whip her kit off so she could paint her. Preferably lying in the bath with her arms crossed over her naked breasts and strewn with rose petals. Far better to give her the condensed version.

'A model,' she said. 'Long time ago. Came to a sticky end. Drugs.'

'Sixties, was it?' Emily's eyes were as round as saucers. 'They were all at it in those days, weren't they?'

'Google it later, Em,' Fran replied, cutting Deborah off before she could jump in. 'Deborah, perhaps you could pick up where you left off.'

'Of course. Where was I? Oh yes. So I went outside. It was dark, but there was light coming from the pub, in addition to the fairy lights my friends and I had fixed up around the place to give it a party feel. And then there were the stars of course. The pub used to be an old farm, I think. It's the only way I can explain the muddy old yard you have to walk through to get to it the back way from Little Ware.'

'What time would this have been?'

Deborah thought hard. 'I can't say for certain. This was in the days when eleven o'clock was chucking-out time on a

Saturday night. The pub was still full, so before eleven.'

'Much before?'

'I don't think it could have been much before. We'd sung 'Happy Birthday' and cut the cake. And we'd run out of money for more booze. So I guess it was pretty much time to leave.'

'Okay. What next? You were outside getting some fresh air.'

'I saw three figures in the distance,' Debbie said. 'A guy, and well . . . I'm not sure about this. Could have been two girls, could have been another guy and a girl.'

'What were they doing?'

'I'd say they were arguing. There was a lot of arm-flailing.'

'Could you hear what they were saying?'

Deborah shook her head. 'Too far away. Plus there was music and a lot of noise coming from inside too.'

'Did you get an impression of their ages?'

'Bearing in mind I'd just turned eighteen, I thought they were probably a bit older than me. But then everybody is, practically, when you're that age, aren't they?'

Fran had to agree with that. In the same way that these days most people were younger. Take that chiropractor she had an appointment with. Not a day over thirty, according to Mags. Fully qualified and a partner in her own practice already.

'They all had jeans on. Same sort of height. Though that could have been an illusion. The ground slopes a lot round here,' she continued. 'The one whose gender I couldn't tell was wearing a hoody. The guy was smoking. Weed, I think. I got a whiff of it on the night air. One of them had very blond long hair, which is why I knew at once that she was female. Plus I thought I recognised her.'

'You did?' Emily caught Fran's eye.

'I'm pretty sure it was one of those sisters from the holiday cottage. I used to see them occasionally out and about. They were all blond, tall, sort of *other*.'

'How do you mean, *other*?'

'Different from the locals, I suppose. With one or two notable exceptions hereabouts, we're all mostly small and dumpy. Peasant stock, I suppose. I include myself in that description.' She grinned broadly.

'You can't be any more specific about which of the sisters it was, could you?' Fran said.

Deborah shook her head. 'The youngest one, I think. Carola, she was called, wasn't she?'

Fran and Emily exchanged a glance. Were they finally getting somewhere at last?

'You've done very well to remember so much after such a long gap of years,' Fran said.

'The artist's eye,' Deborah replied proudly. 'I guess it's not so very different from that of a detective's, Sergeant.'

If only, Fran thought. She liked to think her own memory for detail was as strong as it always had been, but since the accident she was prone to moments of confusion — usually, like now, when she was struggling to make some sort of connection between so many disparate pieces of information.

On the face of it, the case should have been a simple one. A child goes missing from its bed in the middle of the night. Snatched right from under the noses of her parents and a houseful of aunts, friends, and acquaintances. How could it be possible without somebody seeing something?

Where was this case going? Was it going anywhere at all? Her thoughts turned to Betty Taverner, estranged from her daughter, living in a tumbledown old cottage yet in possession of a car that was out of the reach of most people's finances. Wasn't there something fishy about that, not to mention her certainty that the man she'd been living with at the time of Emma-Jane's disappearance had had nothing to do with her disappearance? What made her so sure about that, unless she knew who *had* been responsible? Only days ago, Tony Best had been heard crying Emma-Jane's name out in his sleep. Why would he do that unless he was still troubled by her disappearance?

And now there was Carola Rose and the two figures outside the pub. It had been her intention to call on Carola and ask her how much she knew about Best and the dynamics in the cottage at the end of the row, in the hope it might help her piece together some, at least, of the missing jigsaw.

But now she had something much more crucial to ask Carola. Who was that mysterious third person she and her boyfriend been seen arguing with in the back yard of The Hole in the Wall? And what, exactly, had they all been up to?

★ ★ ★

'Damn! No signal!'

Emily, sitting on the boot of the car, glared at her smart phone for some time, but still it refused to oblige. The plan now was to visit Carola before they drove to Fairfax Rise. Cornered, she couldn't very well avoid talking about what Deborah Butcher said she'd seen.

It had been Emily's plan to google the boyfriend's name. Nick d'Arley Gillies, according to the list of names of everyone who'd been present at The Priory the night Emma-Jane disappeared. There couldn't be too many people with a name like that around, she'd reasoned. But unfortunately Emily's precious Google seemed to be letting her down just when she needed it most.

'Try walking over to the top of that hillock,' Fran, already in the car and rummaging through her bag for her painkillers, suggested. 'It might work.'

Emily did so. 'No use,' she said glumly on her return. 'We're going to have to call the nick and get them to find out where d'Arley-Gillies lives these days.'

'Let's leave that pair for now.' Fran swallowed two tablets with half a bottle of water before strapping herself into her seat belt. 'I think we should head off to Fairfax Rise.'

'Why? Surely this is a far better lead?' Emily sounded disappointed.

'You might be right,' Fran said. 'And if you are, then let's not rush in there all guns blazing. The half hour it'll take to get to the Care Home will be a good opportunity to check over Carola and

Nick's statements. Softly, softly catchee monkey, Emily.'

Reluctantly, Emily climbed back into the driving seat, started the car and soon they were off. It took a couple of minutes for Fran to find Carola's statements, three of them in all. She read the original one aloud, to put Emily in the picture as she drove. It stated that on the evening of Saturday the 19th, Emma-Jane had been put to bed by her mother, Aften, just as she had the previous evening. She could state for definite that it was eight o'clock because the church clock chimed the hour and she remembered Aften saying that Emma-Jane's usual bed time was seven-thirty, but that the summer was so short and that it seemed a shame to bundle her off to bed when the weather was lovely.

'So far so straightforward,' Emily said.

Fran continued.

''My boyfriend — Nick d'Arley Gillies — was visiting for the weekend. He wanted to pay a visit to the local pub, The Hole in the Wall, because I'd told him some interesting things about it — not least that it could only be reached through walking through the farmyard to the east of The Priory. So we left just after nine thirty and stayed till eleven',' she read.

'This d'Arley Gillies,' Emily put in, 'does he corroborate this?'

'We'll get to him later.'

'OK. Read me some more of hers.'

Fran obliged. ''We both had two pints of the local brew, played a game of darts, chatted to a couple of the locals whose names I don't remember, and then made our way home back through the farm yard at eleven o'clock when the last orders bell rang.' She's pretty specific about hearing the bell at eleven o'clock. Be interesting to find out if the boyfriend heard it too.'

Fran reached for d'Arley Gillies's statements. Quickly she skimmed through them. 'It's there in all three of his statements.'

'Very convenient,' Emily said. 'But no mention of this third person Deborah Butcher is so certain she saw?'

Fran shook her head. 'None whatso-
ever. Not in any of the statements made
by either of them.'

'You've got to say it sounds a bit
suspicious.'

Fran nodded.

'Listen to this bit,' she said. ' 'We'd
both got mud on our boots and we didn't
want to tramp it into The Priory, so we
went down to the schoolhouse and
cleaned them up with some old rags kept
there for that specific purpose. We stayed
there till about one o'clock in the
morning, drinking. The front door of The
Priory wasn't locked, so we didn't need a
key to get in. Neither of us had occasion
to believe that Emma-Jane wasn't in bed
asleep. It was only the next morning that
we discovered what had happened.'

'Does anything differ from that in
either of her subsequent statements?'

'Let me see.' Fran skimmed quickly
through the second statement. Six years
had passed. 'The only thing that differs
here is that she refers to Nick d'Arley
Gillies as 'my former boyfriend', she said.
'Other than that it's remarkably similar to

the first statement.'

'What about the final one?'

A quick read revealed it to be just the same as the others. 'Almost word for word in fact,' Fran said. 'And if you read her boyfriend's statements, you'll see that all three of his are practically a carbon copy of each other and a word-for-word match for hers.'

'It's like a script they've drawn up together and memorized,' Emily said. 'Most people, when asked to remember something, tend to remember it differently each time. They wouldn't reel it off like these two had.'

Fran agreed. 'I keep trying to remember something Deborah said in passing just now. It's there, flickering about in the corner of my mind. But it won't stay still long enough for me to grab it.'

'It'll come to you when you least expect it,' Emily said. 'That's what usually happens.'

'Yes, you're probably right.'

Funny, but Kev used to say exactly that. Would she ever hear him say it again? she wondered. For a while she was lost in her own thoughts. When she looked out of the window again, she saw they'd arrived at the nursing home at last. Through the iron gates they drove, past the sign that instructed them to drive slowly. There were other signs too — to the bursar's office, to the main house, to the chapel. There was even a sign to the mini-market.

'It's nothing like I imagined,' Emily said, inching along the drive past the manicured lawns.

'I might see if I can put my name down,' Fran joked, spotting a family of three generations sitting beneath the shelter of a tree, the oldest in his wheelchair and the youngest in her buggy. 'There might be a long waiting list for a place like this.'

They parked the car and headed for reception, where they announced themselves. They'd expected a long wait before Susan Jones would be free to come down and meet them. But she was there in less than a minute, a look of grave concern on her face.

'Oh dear,' she said, wringing her hands.

'I didn't foresee this. But poor Mr Best has taken a turn for the worse. The chances of you being able to speak to him now aren't great, but you can try.'

'Well, we've come all this way,' Fran said.

'Of course. Perhaps you'd like to follow me. It's this way. Perhaps we ought to take the lift,' she added with a tactful glance at Fran's stick.

They followed her into the lift, where she pressed the button. 'He's in his room in bed,' she said as the doors closed. 'He has someone sitting with him.'

'His daughter?' Fran asked.

'Well, apparently yes. But I've never seen her before today. This is someone who's never visited before. She signed herself in as Beth Hunt, I believe.'

'Hunt? Not Taverner?' Fran said.

'I don't think so.' Susan Jones thought for a moment. 'No, definitely Hunt. She seemed quite agitated. Insisted she was his daughter and she needed to see him alone because she had something very important to tell him. I told her she could have five minutes, but that I'd be returning very shortly with an officer of the law, and that when I did she'd have to go.'

The lift doors slid open, and they stepped out onto a corridor that was identical to the one they'd just come from. 'Here's his room. Just to the left here.'

The door to Tony Best's room was open. From the doorway, Fran could just about make out the bed where the recumbent figure of Tony Best lay, and a chair to the side of it. Empty.

★   ★   ★

Fran had spent most of the night awake, dragging her aching body from one position to another in a vain attempt to get more comfortable. Round about six o'clock, she'd given up on the idea of sleep completely and decided to get up, have an early breakfast, then go and visit Kev before her appointment with the chiropractor later.

She was updating Kev on the news when Shirelle, one of the nurses, popped her head round the door. She was sorry to interrupt, she said, but she was here to do Kev's obs.

'He could do with a shave,' she said, peering at Kev's bristly face. 'It's been a couple of days since his last one.'

'I could do it,' Fran heard herself volunteer.

'Are you sure?'

How hard could it be? It was a shave, not a tracheotomy.

'Right, Kev, I'm going in,' she said when they were on their own again, Shirelle having dashed off elsewhere. Gripping the razor firmly, she made a start. There was so much dark stubble, and it seemed to be everywhere, lurking in all the crevices of his face.

'That Carola Rose and the boyfriend. It's making me think, Kev,' she said as she worked. 'No mention of a third person, not in Carola's statements or any of the boyfriend's either. Suspicious, don't you think?'

She paused to appraise her work. She studied him for so long that she began to imagine some movement in his face — a flickering eyelid, a twitch in the corner of his mouth. But no, that was impossible. Dismissing it as a fantasy, Fran continued with her story.

'Emily thought so too. She was itching to get back in the car and go and look for her. Good job we didn't though, because we'd never have found her at her old address. *And* we'd have missed the other business in the hospital.'

The scratch of the razor against Kev's cheek was oddly soothing.

'She's living in London now, apparently. The ex-boyfriend too.' She gave a sigh. 'You know what London means, don't you, Kev? Not our beat, so we've had to give it to the Met.'

How had Debbie Butcher described the locals? *Peasant stock*, that was it. *With one or two notable exceptions.* Who *were* the notable exceptions? she wondered. Betty Taverner had been tall once upon a time, till age and hard work had shaved off a couple of inches from her height. Tall mothers generally had tall children, didn't they? Recalling their visit to Betty's crowded cottage, she recalled there was not one picture of her daughter there. Was *she* tall? Fran wondered.

This Beth Hunt, Tony Best's visitor — she *had* to be Beth Taverner. There was no other explanation. But how had she known where to find him? Had Betty Taverner relayed the information Fran herself had given her?

So many questions, but no answers. Fran had left Emily with the task of finding an address for Beth Hunt. If she failed to get anywhere before Fran left the chiropractor's after her appointment later this morning, then she'd need no persuading to drive back over to Little Ware, corner Betty Taverner and threaten her with the full weight of the law unless she revealed where they could get hold of the daughter she said she'd broken off contact with years previously.

She'd become so taken up with this train of thought that she must have allowed her concentration to slip. Just a second was all it took for the razor to make a nick in Kev's chin.

When a bead of bright red blood rose to the surface, she gasped at the intensity of its colour. It couldn't be true that Kevin was that dreadful thing she'd overheard colleagues back at the nick say he was — a cabbage. Not if red blood could still flow from his veins. Cabbages didn't bleed.

'Oh, if only you'd damn well wake up and tell me off for being so careless!'

She dabbed away at the blood furiously, tears pricking her eyes. Then she saw it again. A flicker at the corner of his mouth. It disappeared as quickly as it had arrived. But there was no mistaking it. The sound of the door opening behind her made her jump. Shirelle was back.

'I'm sorry if I made you jump.' She drew closer to the bed. 'You've done a fine job,' she said, peering at Kev's now smooth face.

'Apart from slicing off a piece of his chin,' Fran replied.

She was tempted to mention what she was certain she'd seen, but already she could anticipate Shirelle's answer. How often had she heard one or other of the nurses say that friends and relatives frequently imagined they saw movement where there was none at all?

'I know you'd like to stay,' Shirelle said. 'But there's a colleague of yours outside. I said I'd come and get you.'

News at last. She should have welcomed it, but what she longed to do was stay here by Kev's side, just in case he showed more signs of life.

'No rest for the wicked,' she said, reluctantly getting up. 'So what on earth *you're* doing here, taking up somebody's bed who *really* deserves a rest, I've no idea.'

It was a bad joke. But it *was* a joke. Her way of coping. She bet Kev knew that, even if he couldn't acknowledge it.

★   ★   ★

As soon as she caught sight of Fran, Emily rushed towards her. 'You'll want to hear this,' she said. 'More news from Fairfax Rise. I'm afraid Tony Best is dead.'

'When?'

'Sometime in his sleep. One of the carers found him when she went to take

82

him breakfast this morning. She said we might be interested in something he said to her before she left his room last night.'

'We'd better get over there, then,' Fran said.

She did her best to keep up with Emily as they made their way through the labyrinthine corridors and out to the hospital exit. For her part, Emily did her best to slow down, so that a casual onlooker might be forgiven for imagining the two women walked at the same pace.

'I'm sorry I took so long with Kev,' Fran said once they were in the car and she was strapping herself in. 'I only meant to pop in and say hi.'

'No need to apologise. I think it's wonderful, the way you refuse to give up on him.'

Fran didn't want to get into a discussion about her relationship with Kev. Especially since she'd be hard pressed to explain it even to herself. 'Any news on Carola Rose and d'Arley Gillies?' she said, deftly skirting the subject.

Emily made a face. 'Well, if there is, the Met's not sharing,' she grumbled. 'Not that *that* should come as a surprise. Selfish lot.'

Fran smiled. 'You're far too young to be so cynical. I'm sure they'll be in touch when they've got something to share.'

Emily rolled her eyes to show exactly how likely she thought that was.

'Anyway, maybe once we've spoken to Tony Best's carer, we'll be able to tell *them* something. Who needs the Met, anyway? They're not the only ones who know how to solve an unsolvable case.'

⋆ ⋆ ⋆

Ilona Patric was small, dark and, after her long shift, clearly exhausted. She'd been at Fairfax Rise three months, she said, and loved the old people, though she knew how difficult that was for some — English people in particular, she added — to understand.

'Tony was assigned to me when his daughter brought him in a couple of weeks ago,' she said. 'She has young children as well as him to look after, and needs a break sometimes.'

'You spoke to her then?' Fran wanted to know.

'Oh yes, of course. How else do I find out the things I need to know about him — practical things he perhaps wouldn't want to tell me himself? Old people can be very proud.'

'The name of this daughter was — ?'

'I just know her as Tina.'

'And his other daughter, Beth Hunt?'

'I'd never heard of her before,' she said. 'Not till Tony spoke about her. He told me they'd lost touch years ago when his relationship with her mother broke up. He said he never thought he'd see her again. He was so happy.' Ilona dug her hands into the pocket of her overall. She drew out a photograph and handed it to Fran. 'He showed me this photo,' she went on. 'Told me it was her picture. Beth. She's with his granddaughter who he hadn't seen since she was six years old.'

Fran studied the photograph. It showed a woman in her forties, tall, blond, smiling and attractive, arm in arm with a younger version of herself, smiling just as broadly. Flipping the photograph over, she read the words *Beth and Emma, Christmas 2013*.

'I forgot about it till this morning when I had to strip Tony's bed,' Ilona said. 'It was under his pillow. There was this, too.'

'This' was a business card. It bore the name Taylor and Major, Chiropractors. Wasn't that the practice she was booked into later that morning? If she'd booked her appointment herself, she'd have remembered the name. But this was the thing. *She* hadn't made the appointment at all. That had been her friend Mags's doing. When Fran had let slip that the physio sessions she'd been having didn't seem to be helping much, Mags had given her the details of her chiropractor. Fran had meant to make the call, but she'd never got round to it.

That was when Mags, exasperated by Fran's lack of action, had jumped in and done it for her. Then she'd handed her the appointment card telling Fran where, when and what time to turn up. The card had been sitting on her mantelpiece for the last week until this morning, when she'd grabbed it before leaving the house and shoved it in her jacket pocket.

Now she drew it out and scrutinised it. It was virtually identical to the business card Ilona had just given her. It was with a thrill of excitement that she read the name of the chiropractor Mags had made her an appointment to see. *Emma Taylor* — same name as the one on the card Ilona had found under Tony's pillow.

She flashed both cards at Emily, whose eyes widened as soon as she'd taken in the information. Fran knew she must be thinking the same thing she was thinking herself. Could the Emma in the photograph and this chiropractor who called herself Emma Taylor be Emma-Jane Maltby?

'What else did Tony say about his granddaughter?' Fran asked Ilona.

'That she was a partner in the practice. And that she was married now. He was very proud. Very happy.'

He would be, Fran mused. *Any man would.*

'But sad too,' Ilona said. 'Because of all the lost years he didn't spend with them.'

Fran slipped the photo and cards back in her pocket. 'You've been very helpful, Ilona,' she said. Turning to Emily, she added, 'What was that you were saying earlier? About the Met not being the only ones with the ability to solve an unsolvable case?'

Emily was already out of her seat. 'Let's go,' she said.

* * *

In the car to the chiropractic centre, Fran and Emily agreed that they'd just had the most tremendous piece of luck. But they couldn't get cocky. Beth Hunt could just have been spinning her father a yarn to make him feel better about the grand-daughter he'd lost contact with. This Emma Hunt might not be who they wanted it to be at all. Anybody could pick up a business card, and Emma was a very common name.

'A lot more common than Emily,' Emily cheekily added as they drew up outside Taylor and Major's Chiropractic Centre.

Once inside, Fran gave her name to the receptionist. She had an appointment here after all, though she was twenty minutes late. The idea that any moment now she might come face to face with the young woman they'd been looking for for twenty-five years filled her with anticipation. She could barely contain her patience as the receptionist wasted another minute consulting her appointment book. Her expression, when she next raised her head, was apologetic.

'Miss Phoenix. I'm so sorry,' she said. 'I'm afraid we've had to cancel you for today. Didn't you get the message I left on your phone this morning?'

'Message? No.'

It was her habit to switch off her phone as soon as she entered Kev's room at the hospital, and this morning had been no exception. She must have forgotten to switch it back on.

Now she did. Yup! There was the message from the practice. There were a couple more numbers, too, that she thought she recognised: one from her connection at the Met, and the other from the hospital. Why were *they* ringing? Had Kev taken a turn for the worse? She was filled with a deep sense of foreboding.

'You were booked in with Emma, weren't you? Emma Taylor. Sadly she had a bereavement in the family only this morning. Her grandfather died.'

Fran blinked at the receptionist. Her words seemed to reach her from a long way off. She struggled to get her focus back. This was what she'd wanted, wasn't it? A result. But all she could think about was the message from the hospital she was far too afraid to listen to.

Thankfully, Emily wasn't to be so easily sidetracked. Sensing the sudden change in Fran, she took over. 'You say her grandfather died? Where?'

'An old people's home. Fairfax Rise, I think it's called. He died his sleep, I believe.'

'Right. Thank you. You've been very helpful. And now will you kindly give me an address for her?'

⋆ ⋆ ⋆

90

It was Emily who'd listened to the message on Fran's phone too, in the end. It had taken a while for the significance of her great big grin to register with Fran, so certain was she that the news could only be bad. Kev had showed signs of movement, apparently, and Fran should get there as soon as she could.

Driving like a demon, the blue lamp flashing all the way, Emily had deposited her outside Kevin's wing of the hospital before driving off to relay the information about Emma to the rest of the team.

When she'd found her way to his room, Kevin's bed had been surrounded by white coats. As soon as she spotted Fran, Shirelle slipped out from among the group and came towards her, grinning from ear to ear. Kev was back in the land of the living, she announced. Half an hour after Fran had left, he'd opened his eyes fully.

Since then, he'd made more progress. He hadn't spoken yet, she said, but they were sure he would. And there was movement in his fingers, too; he'd gripped the doctor's hand hard when he'd asked him to squeeze it tight. Best of all, he was breathing on his own.

So it really *was* true — Fran hadn't imagined those movements she'd seen earlier that morning when she'd been shaving him! A couple of hours had passed since then. During that time, Fran had managed to listen to her other message, from her contact in the Met. And what she'd heard was very interesting. Emily had got back to her too. It seemed that finally all the pieces had fallen into place.

The white coats had all left apart from one, who was on his way out. 'You're the one who comes by most days, right?' he said. 'The nurses say you never run out of things to say to him.'

She nodded. 'I've got even more stuff to tell him now,' she said.

The doctor smiled at her. 'I'd better leave you to it, then,' he said. At the door, he gave her a wave and then he was gone, leaving her alone with Kev.

She went and sat next to his bed, marvelling at the fact that most of the equipment she was used to seeing had disappeared. Was he sleeping, or was he up to his old trick of feigning sleep just to get a bit of Kev time?

'I've got some good news, Kev,' she whispered. 'Emma-Jane's alive. She's dropped the hyphen and the Jane and she's swapped the Maltby for Taylor.'

She paused, hoping for some reaction, but none came. Undeterred, she ploughed on.

'Course, she'd never really been a Maltby in the first place. We should have guessed that years ago. But we missed it. She was Beth Taverner's daughter, born when Beth was just fifteen.' She sighed. 'Given away by Betty, she was, who didn't want the shame of it. Poor Beth had no say in the matter. Can you imagine that, Kev?'

Not even given away, though. Sold. For a huge sum of money to Aften Rose and her husband, who couldn't have children of their own. Had Aften and Josh Maltby believed Betty Taverner when she told them Beth was handing over her baby of her own free will? Or had they simply turned a blind eye because it suited them?

Of course, when Emma-Jane disappeared, they must have thought that losing her was their punishment for taking the infant away from her birth mother.

Fran thought about the BMW parked outside Betty Taverner's cottage. *She* was still living off the profits of her dreadful deed. Not surprising Beth had cut her off and Tony Best had washed his hands of her. Though maybe Betty Taverner had had *some* feelings in the end, letting Beth know that the man she'd once called daddy was dying in an old people's home.

'We got there before them, the Met boys, you'll be happy to hear,' she said. 'Though them, finding Carola Rose and her ex-boyfriend went some way to putting the rest of the jigsaw together.'

When confronted with the evidence that they'd been seen with a third party the night Emma-Jane disappeared, those two had no choice but to confess how they'd smuggled the sleeping Emma-Jane out of her room and into her real mother's car waiting at the back of the cottage, she told Kev.

'When Debbie Butcher saw the three of

them chatting together behind the pub, they must have been discussing how best to go about it. It certainly chimes with the boyfriend's confession. He never wanted to get involved, he said. Insisted the two women bullied him into keeping watch while they smuggle Emma-Jane and her stuff out of the house. Of course, then he was implicated and couldn't very well go to the police and own up to his part in it. *She* said she'd do it again under the same circumstances. You've got to admire her loyalty, but she'll be facing charges for perverting the course of justice just like he will. Then there's the small matter of buying and selling the baby in the first place. I'd like to see what the courts will make of that!'

Kev stirred. Opened his eyes. Blinked a few times. He stared at her for some time, as if he was trying to work out who she was.

'Kev?' she said. 'It's Fran.'

Kev cleared his throat. And then he spoke, his voice rusty with lack of use. 'What you having, Fran?' he said. 'Nice glass of Pinot Grigio, is it?'

It took a second for Fran to work out that Kev had travelled back in time to the moment before they'd crashed. These were the very last words he'd spoken to her before they'd both lost consciousness.

'I'm not sure we can get one of those in here,' she replied, keeping her voice as steady as she could under the circumstances. 'What about a nice cup of tea instead? And then I've got something I really want to tell you.'

Two things actually. The first was the story of Emma-Jane Maltby, who had disappeared in 1989 and was found alive and well twenty-five years later. Because as usual with Kev, he hadn't been listening the first time.

The second . . . Well, that might prove to be a bit more awkward. How did you tell someone you thought you loved them when you'd never said it before? She was going to have to think about that one.

THE KNOCK
AT THE DOOR

Caroline closed the study door behind her and sat down in front of her computer. She just had time to dash off a few words to Mark. He looked forward to her emails so much, he'd often said. Though really she couldn't think why. All she ever did was witter on about the house.

How naïve she'd been when she'd first put in an offer for Dovecoats, this sprawling old mansion in the middle of nowhere that was now their home. Back then, she'd imagined all that needed to be done was to paint a few walls, lay a few carpets, perhaps replace the draughty windows with double glazing. Nothing that would cause too much disruption to family life.

She'd had no idea just how long and how complicated it would turn out. It wasn't finished even now, two years on. Her list of things to do was still longer than the list of things that had been completed. But despite that, already it was home. And in two months now Mark would be back for good, able to share it with them.

At least she had some proper news today — albeit news that would make Mark as sad as it had made the rest of them. Her fingers flew over the keyboard as she related the tale of poor Slipper's demise. A natural death in the end, not the one she'd dreaded having to explain to the children. The visit to the vet and the needle, because it wasn't fair to make poor Slipper linger any longer with all those ailments that had been making his life so difficult for so long.

She was going to have to trek over there shortly, to make sure there was no bickering going on among them. The boys had jumped at her suggestion that they should be in charge of digging the grave, flattered that she thought them strong enough and sensible enough too to take on such an important task.

Actually, they were all being marvellously grown up about it, not just the older two. There was something about Slipper's death that had lent dignity to every single member of her little brood, even including Sam, who wouldn't be eight till next month. It was Sam who'd insisted on bearing poor Slipper's body, wrapped up in his favourite rug, all the way from the house down to the bluebell wood, the spot they'd unanimously agreed on as his last resting place.

Carys had spent most of this morning writing a speech to deliver at the graveside. Possibly a poem. A funeral was exactly the sort of dramatic occasion she revelled in. Caroline bit her lip, worried at the prospect of the effect one of Carys's poems might have on the two older boys, who were noted for their ability to find humour in most things.

'Be kind to her. Remember she's only ten and she can sometimes get carried away,' she'd told them as she'd helped them pile up the wheelbarrow with all the tools they'd need to dig a grave deep enough and worthy enough for the dog who'd been their constant companion for all of their fourteen years.

'Darling,' she wrote, conscious that time was pressing and she really ought to be making a move, 'I'm so sorry you can't be here for the wake. We're having sausage rolls and lemonade, and Carys helped Mrs Banks make a cake in the shape of a bone. She wanted a dog-shaped cake of course, but Mrs Banks did that thing with her mouth — you know, where she makes it disappear — and, well, that was the end of that.'

The clatter of footsteps running up the stairs startled her. Goodness! Did they have to make such a racket! Already she was regretting not laying carpet on the stairs. She leapt up from her seat, marched over to the door and flung it open.

'I said I'd be there soon, didn't I?' she called out.

At the bottom of the stairs, four pairs of startled eyes stared up at her. The two older boys were red in the face, their cheeks streaked with dirt, their clothes filthy from all that digging. Sam's beautiful mouth in his angelic face was a wide O. It was Carys, her hand clutched to her heart, who spoke.

'Mummy, you're going to have to come and see. There's a skeleton buried right in the spot where we were going to bury Slipper. A fully grown human one.'

★　★　★

'I've brought cakes.' Detective Sergeant Sal Jones, newly appointed head of Strapley County's cold case investigation team, dropped the box onto the middle of the table with casual aplomb.

'You've got a good team,' the super had said last week after he'd congratulated her on her promotion. 'But watch out for Paddy Bradshaw. He's bound to hold a bit of a grudge because he didn't get the job and you did.'

If this warning was the super's way of keeping her on her toes, then she didn't know how she felt about it. Sal swept the table with a razor gaze. Already she'd picked him out, thanks to the super's description. *Always looks like he's about* to burst into tears. *Has a bit of a problem with technology. Cracks his knuckles a lot, which some people find a bit irritating.* He'd said it like *he* was one of those people.

He'd filled her in about Keris Brewster, too. *Twenty-five. Don't be fooled by her penchant for pink. She's as sharp as a tack,* he'd said. Sal had already noticed the pink fluffy pencil case. She found it oddly touching. Like it was the start of the new term and Keris was out to impress Miss. And in her favour, she was the only one in her new team who'd smiled at her.

'Then there's Frazer Clarkson. Mid-thirties. Dark horse, that one. Thinks a lot.'

The super had failed to mention Frazer's good looks. He looked like a man who ran. Slick, sleek. When she suggested everyone dug in and grabbed a cake, he bestowed a look of disdain on the contents of the box. Maybe she should have brought pumpkin seeds instead.

Or perhaps she should have brought nothing at all. She was suddenly gripped by a feeling of self-loathing. What was it about her that she felt that in order to do her job properly, she needed to be liked? She was their superior, wasn't she? That should be enough.

'So,' she said once the cakes had disappeared, apart from the one Frazer had turned his nose up at. Sal licked the icing sugar from her fingers and tried to ignore the pinch of her belt at her waist. 'This new case.'

The police and SOCO had been called a fortnight ago to Dovecoats, a large recently renovated property in the village of Lampleigh in its own grounds and currently owned by Doctor and Mrs Buckley, she told them. 'He's overseas at the moment somewhere in Africa. A doctor. So it's just Mrs Buckley and the children living there. It was the kids that found the body, actually — or rather the skeletal remains. Apparently they were digging a grave for their dead dog.'

There was an exchange of glances around the table and some shuffling of feet and papers. Sal caught Keris's eye and could have sworn she saw her lips twitch. Sal passed round the photos SOCO had taken at the scene.

'The skeleton was established to be that of a male, probably around twenty-five or so, about five-ten with an old fracture to the left wrist but no obvious signs of blunt force trauma,' Sal said. 'There were no personal belongings found on or near the body. As you can see, it was partially wrapped in a rug, but most of that was rotted through.'

'Cause of death?'

'That's still being investigated. We might never know till we find out who killed him.'

'Do we even know who he is?' Keris asked.

Sal shook her head. 'If we can't identify him from his DNA or dental records, we might have to push for a facial reconstruction. You never know, someone out there might recognise him from the digital images once they've been circulated in the media.'

Frazer Clarkson let the photograph he was holding drop. 'So what do we do now?' he said, looking directly at Sal.

'We dig. Find out who owned the house before the present family. Visit this Mrs Buckley, talk to the children.'

'I'm up for that.'

'We'll go together,' Sal said, rising from her chair.

'What about us?' Paddy Bradshaw said. He sounded rather peeved, Sal thought.

Keris dipped into her briefcase to retrieve her laptop, which she opened and began to immerse herself in, clearly disassociating herself from him.

'Well, you could start checking on missing persons. Any time between 1980 and 1990.' That should take him till lunchtime, Sal mused.

'I'm already on it,' Keris said.

Well, at least she could trust one of them to keep themselves busy when she wasn't there.

'And if Frazer doesn't want his cake, do you mind if I have it?' Keris glanced longingly at the remaining one. 'Unless you want it, Paddy, of course? Or we could share it.'

Paddy shook his head. 'Be my guest.'

Sal grinned as Keris grabbed it. She

decided was going to enjoy working with DC Brewster. Though she could envisage some fights ahead over the biscuit tin.

★ ★ ★

'Nice family.'

The two of them were strolling down the long drive back to the car. Frazer had driven them to Dovecoats without even asking if it was okay with her. Now he got back in on the driver's side, leaving Sal to open her door for herself. She was glad about that. Chivalry was fine on a night out, but at work she was incapable of seeing it as anything other than some man doing his best to put her in her place.

'They are,' he said, switching on the ignition.

'That little girl took a real shine to you.'

Come on Clarkson, give me something, Sal thought as she strapped herself in. He'd been as keen as mustard up there at the house, peering curiously into the grave, which was still a crime scene surrounded by tickertape, listening attentively to the children argue about who had been the first to spot the skeleton after they'd dug as deep as they could for a grave for poor old Slipper so the foxes wouldn't get him. He'd been charming to Mrs Buckley too, drinking her tea — though admittedly passing on her biscuits, admiring her house, even asking if the painting on the wall was by who he thought it was. Apparently it was, and Mrs Buckley had been thrilled that he'd recognised it.

Sal knew nothing about art. She didn't even know what she liked. She'd actually felt quite stupid sitting there like piggy in the middle while they discussed painting techniques and how the artist who'd painted the picture on her wall may have gone out of fashion but it didn't matter because they both still loved his work. Sal had eaten rather a lot of biscuits while that little conversation had been going on.

But now, driving along, Frazer had lapsed into silence, barely acknowledging her remark about little Carys and how taken she'd been with him, even slipping her hand into his as she'd led them down to the spot in the wood where they'd unearthed the human remains. Mrs Buckley had apologised profusely for her daughter's familiarity, explaining to Carys that he was a police officer not a friend. But it hadn't stopped the little girl resolutely holding fast to Fraser's hand. And he'd done nothing to free it.

Oh damn it. She was going to have to start a conversation if he wouldn't. 'Have you got kids, Fraser?' she asked. 'You seemed to know how to talk to them.'

His eyes didn't move from the road ahead. 'I have, as a matter of fact. A little girl. Same age as Carys.'

'That's nice.'

'It's not, actually. She lives with her mother. I don't see enough of her. Not even every other weekend. Not with this job and these hours.'

'I'm sorry,' Sal muttered, adding after a pause during which she struggled to find something to say he wouldn't find even more intrusive, 'You're right, though, about us being in the wrong job to start a family. I've been telling my old man the same for years. And now we're both too old to start.'

'Do you mind about that?'

Now who was being intrusive? 'Nah! We're both far too set in our ways to have our lives disrupted,' she replied, probably rather too forcefully.

They didn't speak again till they'd arrived at their next stop, Palmer's Court, the current home of Eleanor Godley. Caroline Buckley had informed them that Miss Godley had lived at Dovecoats from the early sixties right up until three years ago, when she'd sold it to the Buckleys.

Palmer's Court was no ordinary old people's home of the kind run by local councils, purpose-built and utilitarian. In fact it was a veritable village. It crossed Sal's mind that you had to be seriously wealthy to be able to afford to live here. As they drove along the leafy avenue to the main block, she spotted signs to the spa, the gym and the library. It was smarter than some hotels she'd stayed in.

Eleanor Godley cut an imposing figure sitting straight-backed in her winged leather chair by the window of her room, which looked out onto a pleasant view. She apologised for not getting up to greet them, pointing to her stick as the reason. When they'd rung through to tell her the police were here to have a word with her, she'd been so excited, she said, her pale eyes twinkling in her deeply wrinkled yet still beautiful face. From the photographs sitting on top of her display cabinet, it was clear that as a younger woman she had been stunning.

'What have I done wrong, Inspector?' she said, her voice ringing with the authority of her class. 'Are you going to cart me off in handcuffs? I do hope so! Life can be a bit too quiet these days.'

It was impossible not to be drawn to the old lady. Even her initial assumption on meeting them that Frazer was the superior officer hadn't riled Sal. Most ninety-five-year-olds would have probably made a similar assumption. She continued to address her remarks to him and not to Sal, but Sal was happy enough to sit back and admire the décor. Plus it gave her the opportunity to see Frazer at work again. From what she'd observed of him so far, it seemed he was either totally on or totally off. Right now, he was totally on; and Eleanor Godley, just like Caroline Buckley before her, was lapping up the charm, tilting her head coquettishly as she listened to Frazer explain why they were here.

'The present owner couldn't lay her hands on the deeds of the house when we were there. Thinks they're probably with the solicitor,' he explained. 'But she says you lived at Dovecoats for a long time. That you only moved out about three years ago, in fact.'

'That's right,' the old lady said. 'It was with a great deal of regret that I had to leave my beloved home.' She looked suddenly deflated. 'I spent more than fifty years of my life there. Moved there in 1963. You can imagine the memories it holds for me.'

Did that include bashing someone's brains out and shoving him six feet under the ground? Sal wondered. She might be an old lady now, but a glance at those photos of her in various poses showed someone tall and strong, capable of a

111

great deal. If she'd had an accomplice, who knew what they might have achieved between them?

'I can indeed imagine,' Frazer said. To Sal's amazement he leaned forward and took Miss Godley's hand in his. 'But if it's any consolation,' he went on, 'now the house is full of children who I'm sure will make lots of wonderful memories for themselves in their turn.'

My goodness, but he was good!

'Alas, Inspector, I had no husband and no children either. I was a career woman in the days when you could either have one or the other.'

Sal had had rather enough of this display of affection. Not to mention the fact that Eleanor Godley appeared to have promoted Frazer Clarkson, a mere DS, to inspector. It was time to step in.

'Miss Godley,' she said, 'we believe that the remains we found on your property — your ex-property — were of someone, a man, who died, probably murdered, some time between 1980 and 1990. You were living there then, weren't you?'

'Well, yes, we've already established

that,' she said. 'But if you're implying that I had anything to do with it . . . '

'Of course not,' Frazer jumped in. 'But we do need to ask — did you ever let the property at any time? Perhaps you went travelling? It was a long time ago.'

'Not to me, Inspector,' she said. 'It only seems like yesterday.' A dreamy expression crossed her face. 'Although I did travel a lot, actually. But never for long. I had my career to think of, you know.'

'What was the longest period of time you ever went away for?' Sal said.

She answered immediately, without the slightest hesitation. 'The summer of '85. I was away from June to September, travelling through Europe.'

'And did you lock up your house?'

'Good heavens, no. I couldn't leave it empty. There'd been a spate of burglaries in the area. So I asked my godson to move in and keep an eye on the place.'

Game on! Sal glanced across at Frazer and they locked eyes. They had a lead.

★   ★   ★

His phone rang just as he emerged onto the airless street from the cool of the high-rise block of offices where he worked. It'd been a long, exhausting day, and he needed a beer before he could even think about tackling the Underground. When his mobile buzzed in his pocket and he saw Eleanor's name flash up, his initial thought was to reject it.

But she was his godmother, and she was old and rich. Maybe she was about to summon him to her deathbed and bestow her fortune upon him before she snuffed it. Then he could retire, buy a boat and sail round the world. Even if she was still in the best of health, it might be worth five minutes of small talk to remind her of his existence.

'Eleanor,' he said in his most caring voice. 'How the hell are you?'

'Oh never mind all that, Oscar.' Her voice was muffled, far away. But she sounded excited. 'The police have been here. Somebody's remains have been discovered in the grounds of Dovecoats.'

At first he didn't think he'd heard her

right. When he knew he had, he began to feel sick. He stopped walking and took himself to the side of the road, where he leaned against the wall of a building.

'They wanted your address. But I said I didn't have it.'

Up ahead, he saw a pub sign. The Skull and Crossbones. The name was almost funny, except it was anything but.

'Why on earth not, Eleanor?' He spoke with bravado. 'It's not as if I have anything to hide.'

'Of course not, dear,' she said. 'But I just felt I wanted to speak to you before they did.'

'That's very considerate of you.'

'I just don't want you to be surprised when you hear that knock on the door, that's all.'

The knock on the door. How could he tell his godmother that actually, it wouldn't be a surprise to him at all? That actually, he'd been expecting it for more than half his life? The surprise was only that it had taken them so long.

★   ★   ★

115

Right now he couldn't think straight. He'd intended to have one beer. But one beer had led to another, and then he'd felt the compulsion to smoke even though he hadn't smoked in five years. So then he'd had to find a shop that sold cigarettes. The nearest had been next to another pub, so of course he went in.

Cressida wasn't talking to him now. Though she had a funny way of showing it. Chewing his ear off about what a bad father he was. Telling him he was going to have to have a word with Abigail about her prom dress before she went to bed.

He supposed he'd agreed that he would. But for the life of him, he had no idea what he was supposed to say to a daughter who'd fixed her sights on wearing a dress that was, in the words of his wife, 'Something you'd be more likely to see in a nightclub than at an end of a Year 11 school prom.'

That had been two hours ago. Now he was upstairs in his study, the door shut fast against the world. Cressida thought she was punishing him by telling him she'd thrown his dinner away because it had dried up. But since he had no appetite for food, she'd actually done him a favour.

What he really wanted was a cigarette and a drink. But the first would provoke anther row with Cressida, and the second was out of the question. Right now he needed to keep a clear head.

He'd already decided, once he'd found himself on the commuter train — God only knew how he'd got there! — that the first thing he had to do was get in touch with the others and warn them. But how? He hadn't laid eyes on any of them since they'd parted ways all those years ago. Apart from Ally, of course. Her number was on his phone. But wouldn't it look suspicious if he called her? The police could take your phone and go through your calls. Convict you on them.

Sure, Ally was his sister, and a man was entitled to call his sister ten times a day if he wanted. But he never wanted. He hadn't called her ever. That was Cressida's department. Not even after Abigail had been born had he got in touch to relay the news. He'd left all that to his mum and dad.

Way back, Ally and he had forged an unspoken agreement that the less they had to do with each other, the better. Now they managed just once a year at Christmas when the house belonging to whoever was hosting it that year was full of people and all they had to do was nod at each other across the room and wish each other season's greetings.

He suddenly remembered Facebook. Everyone was on Facebook these days. Even himself. He opened his laptop and clicked on the bookmarked site, then on his own page. There he was. Oscar Ferguson. Lives in: Surrey. From: London. Apparently he had thirty-three friends — two of whom were his immediate family.

In fact, it was one of them — Cressida — who'd insisted he joined. That way he could keep an eye on Abigail and make sure she wasn't being groomed by a paedophile or taking unsuitable selfies. Of course, as soon as he'd sent her a friend request she'd blocked him, so that had been the end of that.

He should try Henry first. But what the hell was his surname? How could he have forgotten it? Hal had been his best mate all through secondary school. They'd rarely been apart. The more he struggled to dredge it up from his tired memory, the more stubbornly it refused to allow him. He was breaking out in a sweat again. At this rate, the stress would kill him.

He told himself to calm down, breathe, and think about something else. It was a technique he'd read about somewhere. Stop trying to remember, and whatever it is you've forgotten will pop into your head when you least expect it.

He could remember *her* name, all right. Hal's girlfriend. Tamara Elegant. Tammy. Tam. How many of those were there on Facebook? he wondered. Then he remembered that many women still changed their names when they got married. What if she was now a Smith or a Jones?

Something else stood in his way. In 1985 he'd had a full head of hair, a flat stomach, and he could run up seven flights of stairs without catching his breath. But now look at him, with his paunch and his receding hairline and his whole future behind him.

Had time been as cruel to Tamara Elegant? Would he recognise her from her picture even if she'd kept her name? There was only one way to find out. He held his breath, his fingers hovering over the mouse. One click and there she was.

'How the hell can you still look like that?' he breathed when he saw her face. The hair was short now, and maybe a more expensive shade of blond. And yes, there were traces of lines around her eyes and mouth. But she looked damn good for all that. Better than Cressida, who was always trying some diet or other that never seemed to work. Her profile said little, though more than his. Lives: London, he read. Married to . . . No way! Oliver sat up in his chair. It couldn't be. As soon as he saw it written down, he recognized it as the name he'd been struggling to remember. Morrish. Henry Morrish. Of course. So they'd stayed together all those years! Whoever would have thought it? Three kids, by the look of it too. Two sons. A daughter.

Suddenly he was back there at Dovecoats. In the good bit, before it all went wrong. The sun seemed to shine every day back then. The sky was always blue. They drifted through the days, practically living outside, and the lack of routine was a routine in itself.

He was so wrapped up in his memories that it was a while before the sound of his phone ringing penetrated the thick layer of nostalgia in which he'd wrapped himself. When he finally did glance down at the screen, it told him what he didn't want to know. Ally wanted to speak to him.

While he sat there staring at the screen, with only the sound of his breathing and the low hum of his computer for company, there came a sudden eruption of female voices that shattered the stillness. Oh God! Cressida and Abigail again, screaming at each other over that damn prom dress. Oliver put his head in his hands. The oestrogen in this house was just too much. It was killing him.

The yelling grew louder and louder, both of them shouting at once. Then the screeching stopped as abruptly as it had started. But that wasn't the end of it. Now there were footsteps up the stairs. Only Abi could take them at such speed. He heard her opening her bedroom door and slamming it behind her with enough force to take it off his hinges.

He knew exactly what would be coming next, having witnessed it so often before. Meanwhile, he took pleasure in these few short breaths of silence. Then it started. That dreadful noise kids passed off as music these days cranked up to an ear-shattering volume.

'Right. That's it,' he muttered.

He never relished the thought of taking Abigail on, but this time she'd gone too far. When he yanked open his study door, he was surprised to see Cressida on the other side of it. Unsurprisingly, he'd failed to hear her climb the stairs beneath the racket coming from Abigail's room. She looked mad as hell. He took a step back, not wanting to do anything to provoke her. He was already in her bad books.

'Hear that?' she said, yanking her head in the direction of Abi's door. 'I've had it all ruddy day! Now it's your turn.'

He should have switched off his computer before he left the room. He should have closed the door behind him. He never should have given her the opportunity to be suspicious of him in the first place. But if you'd been caught playing away once and then your wife found a picture of a beautiful woman on your Facebook page . . . Well, you were never going to have a leg to stand on, were you?

★   ★   ★

Keris stared at her computer screen and wondered where to start. Search for any males between the ages of twenty and thirty years old who'd gone missing between the years 1980 and 1990, she'd been told. It had to be some sort of test. DI Jones was trying to work out how diligent she was or if she was someone who cut corners. Like that Paddy Bradshaw, who'd sloped off as soon as the boss and Clarkson had left. He'd said something about loose ends that needed tying up from another case he was dealing with. Skiving, more like. Though at least if he wasn't here, she didn't have to put up with him cracking his knuckles like he'd done all the way through the meeting earlier.

There were more than three thousand missing person reports each year. One hundred and ten thousand of them adults. More than half of them male. Even if you subtracted the ones in the wrong age group, you still had something in the region of thirty thousand to search for. Then there were the ones who went missing that no one ever reported. Where did you start looking for them when you didn't even have a name?

It was a relief when, just when she'd got as far as number one hundred and seventy five, a text came through.

We're probably looking at 1985.

Well, hallelujah. She'd have it cracked in no time.

How could his life have unraveled so quickly? Less than twenty-four hours ago, he'd been flirting with that redhead from HR, convincing himself he'd still got it when he succeeded in making her blush. Ahead of him was the Tube and the train ride home to his big house with the Aga and the patio and the plans already passed for an indoor swimming pool for when his bonus came through.

Now look at him. Thrown out of his own home by his wife. Not to mention a wanted man. Any day now the police would come looking for him, asking questions.

Last night he'd booked into a hotel. The air con, such as it was, had rattled constantly, conspiring with the traffic and his own disturbed thoughts to give him a sleepless night. After breakfast, he'd gone shopping and grabbed the first shirt he'd seen in his size, swapping it in the changing room for the smelly one he'd worn the day before that he'd been forced to put back on after his shower. A shower that had proved as inadequate as the hotel breakfast.

It looked all right when he'd tried it on, but once he'd sat down in it he realised it didn't fit properly. The collar was tight and there was a gap between two of the buttons where his flesh peeped through. He had a meeting in ten minutes with that smug American from Fleischmann's. It would be a disaster.

He still hadn't looked at Ally's text message. His wife would have said that procrastination was his middle name. But he had done something about contacting Henry through the link on Tamara's page. He might not have his laptop anymore — he wouldn't have been at all surprised if Cressida had chucked it through his study window once she'd seen Tamara's picture and jumped to the wrong conclusion.

But he did have his smart phone, so he'd been able to get onto Facebook through that. His message had been cryptic. His phone number followed by the four most clichéd words in the book. *We need to talk*.

★ ★ ★

Sal and Clarkson were back from Palmer's Court, both buoyed up by the revelation that Eleanor Godley's godson Oscar Ferguson had stayed at Dovecoats in her absence for a period of three months during the summer of 1985. Although in Frazer's case, you would never have guessed he was celebrating. Obviously, being 'on' for so long had drained him dry. Now he was 'off' again.

But Sal was packing enough adrenalin for both of them. The team sat round the table drinking coffee and sharing their news. According to Miss Godley, Oscar would have been eighteen or nineteen back then; a perfectly lovely, sensible boy who was having a gap year before he went off to read sociology at Essex University. Sadly, Miss Godley had said, she didn't have any contact details for him. He was grown up now, of course — something in compliance, and with a wife and a family, the last she'd heard.

'We're obliged to believe her, of course,' Sal said. She blew on her steaming coffee. Perhaps she should have said that actually these days she was more of a tea drinker. But Keris had been kind enough to stop what she was doing to fetch it, so she didn't want to appear ungrateful. Besides, one fussy eater on the team was plenty.

'You think she's covering something up?' Keris wanted to know.

'I think she's hedging her bets,' Sal said. 'She's a canny old thing. Wouldn't surprise me if she'd been on to him herself. Maybe out of sheer curiosity. Maybe to warn him the police are on to him. We don't really know anything about their relationship.'

It would take no time to get an address for him, even if this Miss Godley was reluctant to pass it on, Paddy said with a crack of his knuckles.

'Don't worry,' Frazer suddenly piped up. 'I've already got one.'

'Good!' Sal smiled at him, wondering whether it might encourage him to smile back. It didn't. She turned her attention to Keris instead.

'Well,' she said, 'the latest news is that we have a facial reconstruction.' She glanced over at Paddy, who was pouring sugar into his coffee. 'Do you want to do the honours, Paddy?'

Paddy gestured towards Keris in a way that suggested he'd be doing her a favour by allowing her the honour. Obviously, he hadn't a clue how to work the ginormous computer screen on the wall behind them. Keris jumped up and brought up the images for them all to see.

At the sight of the 3D face, taken from several different angles, Sal felt a strange dip in her insides. One skeleton was pretty much like another when it came down to it. She even struggled to differentiate between male and female till she got her bearings. But what she was seeing now was the face of a young man. Narrow-jawed, a low brow, a well-shaped nose and thin lips. The hairstyle he'd been given must have been a random guess. A mullet, short at the sides and long at the back. It looked slightly ridiculous, Sal couldn't help thinking. But it was of the time. This was someone's son, maybe someone's brother, someone's lover. *We'll find your killer, lad,* she promised him silently.

'I don't suppose you've got a name for him yet, have you?' she asked Keris. 'That really would make my day.'

'Not yet, but uniform are working on it,' she replied. 'Fifty-five young men between the ages of seventeen and thirty went missing between April and September of 1985. Of those, thirty were reported found, either having returned home or having let it be known that they wanted no further contact with their nearest and — er — dearest.'

'That leaves twenty-five,' Paddy said.

Sal wondered if he was expecting a round of applause for that brilliant deduction.

'Of whom ten were confirmed deceased, either through illness, accident, accidental death or homicide. Relatives of the remaining fifteen will be shown these digital images.'

'Good work, Keris,' Sal said.

Keris beamed at her.

'Well,' Sal said, getting up from the table, 'I don't know about you lot, but I've got a home to go to.'

'Is no one going to pay this Oscar

Ferguson a visit?' Paddy Bradshaw wanted to know.

'I don't think so,' Sal said. 'I think we should give him a couple of days. Let him sweat a bit.'

★ ★ ★

Ally wished they wouldn't put TVs in bars. It was right in her line of vision behind the bar and she couldn't avoid seeing it. All the terrible stuff — the refugees, the terrorists, the politicians windbagging. Apart from herself, the barmaid and half a dozen others sitting alone or in pairs, there was no one else present. No one was watching the damn TV, so why on earth was it on, blaring away?

Ruth was late. She'd said she might be. She was a headmistress now in an independent girls' school, and she rarely got away before six during term time, she'd said, making it clear that Ally was aware what a big cheese she was these days. She must have known that Ally had never even finished college what with everything that had gone on.

'I don't care how difficult it is,' she'd said down the phone. 'You jolly well have to make the effort.'

Ruth wasn't the only one who could inject a bit of authority into her voice. And she wasn't stupid either. She must have put two and two together right away. Thirty-one years it had been since they'd last laid eyes on each other. There was only one reason for them to meet up again. Ruth would have sussed what it was.

A dozen or more people had come through that door since she'd arrived. None of them was Ruth. Telling herself she was jinxing the chance of Ruth being the next person to arrive, she made a determined effort to look away. For something else to do, she picked up her phone.

Inevitably, her thoughts turned to Oscar. Over the last three days, she must have left him a dozen messages, but he hadn't returned any of them. Impulsively, she dialled his number one more time. Straight to voicemail, just like before.

'Oscar. I'm at The Blue Lamp, just off Penny Street. Aldgate's the nearest station. I'm waiting for Ruth. You remember Ruth, of course? It took some detective work but I found her in the end. When she gets here, we're going to have a drink. And a chat. About old times. So if you're in town, I think it would be a jolly good idea if you got yourself over here too. Three heads are better than one and all that. Five would be better of course. Which is where you come in. Henry and that girlfriend of his were your friends, not mine. If you could find them . . . Well, speak later.'

She felt better for doing that. Stronger. More resolute. She was nobody's kid sister. No one's old school chum who'd flunked her 'A' levels and ended up in a dead-end job while her best friend had gone through life winning prizes and nabbing all the best jobs.

Perhaps she dared risk another tonic water. Leaving her coat behind on the seat to save her place, she wandered over to the bar. The television was still on, blaring away. A computer image flashed up onscreen. A man staring straight at her. Narrow-jawed, thin-lipped, eyes that bore straight into you.

'Police today released these digital images of the face of a man believed to be somewhere between the ages of twenty and thirty, whose skeletal remains were found buried in the wood of a country house in the picturesque village of Lampleigh in county of Strapley. They are appealing to any members of the public who might be able to identify the man from these images to contact them on the following number.'

Ally couldn't wait to hear any more. She had to get out of here quick, before she gave herself away.

★ ★ ★

An untidy knot of onlookers had gathered by the side of the road, deep in discussion about the accident that had just occurred. PC Barker, who was dutifully collecting witness statements while the paramedics tended the victim, had been a police officer for six months now, and he still found it disturbing, the pleasure some people got from rubbernecking at an RTA. It was better than a night out for some.

'I thought he was drunk,' one woman said, partly to him, partly to her friend who nodded sagely.

'Really?' PC Barker said, his pencil poised above his notebook.

To his way of thinking, this was mere conjecture. A police officer was duty-bound to report only facts. But when a third person echoed that the man currently lying in the middle of the road being tended by two paramedics had been swaying all over the place before he stepped off the pavement, he concluded there must be something in it. The paramedics would find out soon enough anyway, when they got him inside the ambulance and breathalysed him. He'd taken a look at the victim himself, made him comfortable, stood guard over him and waited for the ambulance to arrive. He could testify that it looked far worse than it was, thankfully.

The victim was still conscious, and

when PC Barker had asked him for his name he'd managed to reply, if a bit faintly. Oscar Ferguson, he'd said. Bloke in a nice suit. Though it was a bit of a mess now, what with all the mud splashes and the blood from his nose.

'I was behind him,' someone else said. 'We were going the same way. I wanted to get past him but he wouldn't let me. Not deliberately, like. But every time I went to pass him, he swayed right into my path. Drunk, obviously.'

Okay. That was four witnesses who'd mentioned the drink. This time he wrote it down.

'We got to the edge of the kerb at the same time,' said the same person, a bloke with such a deep scowl on his forehead it looked like a permanent groove. 'I heard his phone ring. It had this really loud ringtone. U2 I think. I saw him pull it out of his jacket pocket. That's when he stepped out in front of that car. He was looking at the phone instead of the traffic.'

That definitely sounded plausible, thought PC Barker. He'd personally retrieved the victim's smart phone several metres away from where the car had flung him. It was in two bits now, sadly. The poor driver of the car that had clipped him was in even bigger bits. Shaking like a leaf, he was.

One of the rubberneckers said something about how if it were up to him, he'd ban all mobile phones. Several people agreed. By the time PC Barker had collected all his statements, the paramedics had stretchered the victim into the ambulance, which was his cue to jump inside the vehicle himself. He'd have to go with him to the hospital to get a statement, of course. Hopefully by then, the poor driver, sitting with a blanket round his shoulders, would have come out of his shock too. Both of them had had a lucky escape.

The whole incident made PC Barker want to ring the wife and tell her just how much he loved her. You never really knew in this life what the world had in store for you from one day to the next, and that was the truth.

Sal was driving today, and it was Frazer's turn to sit in the passenger seat. She'd left Keris back at the station, hanging on the phone in the hope that there would be a deluge of calls from people saying they recognised the digital images from last night's telly. To Paddy she'd allocated a task that would finally prise him off his posterior, a position he enjoyed a bit too much in Sal's opinion.

She and Frazer were on their way to pay Oscar Ferguson a surprise visit before he set off on his daily commute. The super had nabbed her just as she was leaving instructions for Keris. He'd mentioned something about broadcasting an appeal that would go out on tonight's evening news if they hadn't managed to get a lead before four o'clock. More worryingly, he'd said *she* should be the one to do it. She knew what that meant. Some kid from wardrobe criticising what she was wearing. Somebody else from make-up redesigning her face. People telling her how to stand, where to look, how to speak. Just the thought of it made her feel queasy. That was why she'd insisted on driving today. Concentrating on the traffic would take her mind off it.

'Why else would Ferguson have written this Henry Morrish such an urgent message, unless he really needed to speak to him?' Frazer was obviously thinking aloud.

'Maybe because Cressida Ferguson is right. Maybe he was having affair with Morrish's wife and he'd decided to tell him because she wouldn't,' Sal replied.

'Actually, it's a rhetorical question,' Frazer said, sending her a sidelong look. 'Ma'am,' he added, in case she might think he was overstepping the mark.

Well, they'd know soon enough. Sal cast her mind back to earlier that morning. When they'd knocked on the door of the Fergusons' house, round about seven fifteen, it had been Mrs Ferguson who'd opened it. They'd obviously got her out of bed, and by the look of her she hadn't had a great night's sleep.

The sight of her in her dressing gown

with her hair all tousled and her panda eyes brought to Sal's mind that photograph of Cherie Blair the morning after her husband had won the election that first time. Except Sal hadn't been delivering flowers.

When Sal told her they'd like a word with her husband, she'd pulled the belt of her dressing gown tightly round her middle and announced that she had no idea where he was and frankly she didn't want to know. It was hardly the welcome they'd been expecting.

'Perhaps we can come in for a moment,' Frazer said, switching on the charm.

Of course it worked. Once inside, Sal wondered when Mrs Ferguson was going to ask them what they wanted with her other half. But all she seemed concerned about was relating the tale of how she'd kicked him out after discovering that he'd been contacting some woman on social media. Apparently it wasn't the first time he'd been unfaithful to her, she said as she strode up the stairs ahead of them to reveal what she insisted was 'the evidence'.

She'd led them into her husband's study and showed them the Facebook page on his computer screen. She was a beautiful woman, this Tamara Elegant; there was no denying it. And with a name to match.

But they weren't here to discuss Oscar Ferguson's infidelity, real or imagined. They were here to find out what if anything was the connection between him and the so far unidentified remains of a young man that had been found buried in the grounds of his godmother's house back in the summer of 1985.

She was grateful that Frazer had his listening face on though, nodding in all the right places, and seemingly totally unfazed by Mrs Ferguson's excessive use of colourful expletives to describe her husband's behaviour. It gave her the opportunity to play around on Ferguson's Facebook page. He'd obviously left in a hurry, since he'd not bothered logging out. As soon as she spotted that someone had sent him a private message, she clicked on it.

And there she read it. His first message, We need to talk, was followed by the reply, Don't stress. Stay cool. Then an address and a phone number. The message was from a Henry Morrish. It didn't take her more than one click to piece together that he was married to the attractive woman Mrs Ferguson was accusing her husband of having a fling with. But there was much more to this than some sort of dalliance, Sal was convinced.

Not that it was her business to put Cressida Ferguson out of her misery. Besides, from the way things were heading, it looked like pretty soon Mrs Ferguson would have something much more worrying to think about than mere infidelity.

★   ★   ★

The house that belonged to Henry Morrish was different in style to that of the Fergusons' expensive yet sterile and unimaginative big box of an affair. It was much smaller, for a start; a very old and charming little cottage that seemed to be held up on all sides by various extensions added on at different periods throughout the ages, presumably by various incumbents as and when they could afford it.

It had taken them rather longer to find the Sussex village where Morrish lived than either of them could have anticipated from studying the map. Sal knew it was her fault. She'd ignored the satnav, thinking she knew better than it did, and they'd paid the price.

But at last they'd arrived. Was Oscar Ferguson here too, hiding in one of those extensions, after confessing to his friend about his crime? Sal wondered. After all, he had to be *somewhere*.

Henry Morrish was a handsome man, Sal thought. Even though he was a stone heavier than he should have been, he still sported a full head of hair, and his face was the unlined one of a young man. He'd obviously managed to live a stress-free existence. He led them into the kitchen where the sink was piled high with dirty dishes from the night before.

'We're neither of us very domestic, I'm afraid,' he said. 'My wife's an artist. She's even messier than me.'

He ran an advertising company and he worked from home, he told them, when Frazer asked him what he did. Which was why they'd been lucky enough to catch him, albeit before he'd bothered to shower. You got into bad habits when you worked from home, he said, gesturing ruefully to his scruffy tracksuit.

Chance would be a fine thing, Sal mused. What she wouldn't give for a couple of late starts to her day once in a while. All this dashing about seemed to be taking a much bigger toll on her recently than it used to. Even Jeff had noticed it. He'd taken to packing her off to bed with a mug of cocoa and a promise he'd do the washing up. She hated cocoa, but she was grateful for the attention, she didn't mind admitting.

His wife would be back shortly, Henry Morrish informed them. She was probably picking up a few bits and pieces from the art shop in town, he said, after dropping the kids off at school. 'What's this about anyway?' he said, his gaze shifting from one to the other.

144

'Do you know Oscar Ferguson, Mr Morrish?' Sal asked him.

There was an almost imperceptible flicker of the eyelids, but almost immediately he regained his composure. 'Oscar? Good heavens! Fergie, we used to call him. Haven't seen him in ages.'

Frazer read out the message Oscar had sent him via Facebook followed by Oscar's reply.

'I read that too,' Morrish said. 'I sent him my address. And my phone number. I've been waiting for him to get in touch. But so far I haven't heard a dicky bird. He's not in some sort of trouble, is he?' he said, suddenly all concern.

Sal ignored the question. 'How well do you know him?' she asked.

They'd gone to school together, Morrish replied. They'd been quite close, in fact, at one time. 'But then we both went off to different universities at opposite ends of the country. That was that, I'm afraid. These were the days before social media, remember. And boys didn't write letters except to their mothers. And only that when they wanted money.'

'How well did Oscar know your wife?' Frazer said.

'Tammy? Why do you ask?' He sounded surprised.

'We think he must have found you through looking her up first,' Frazer replied.

'Tamara Elegant. There can't be that many of those on Facebook,' Morrish said.

'So you were part of the same crowd once upon a time?' Sal said.

Morrish looked suddenly wary. 'Well, we were all at school together. Tammy came later when they opened the sixth form to girls for the first time,' he said. 'That's when I found myself spending more time with her and less with him. You know how it goes.' He addressed this last remark in a man-to-man way to Frazer. But if Frazer had known *how it goes*, his expression didn't register it.

The sound of a car pulling up on the gravel outside distracted all three of them. The car door slammed and there were footsteps, then the sound of keys being jammed impatiently in the door. They heard her before they saw her.

'Hal, whose car is that outside? They're going to have to move it, because there's no way I can drag the stuff I've just bought all the way up here from the bottom of the drive.'

A windswept Tamara Elegant, dressed as casually as her husband but to a much smarter effect, stood in the doorway and observed the three people gathered there with a lofty curiosity that suggested she didn't take kindly to visitors who arrived unannounced. Her expression didn't alter even after the introductions had been made and Sal explained why they were here.

She couldn't imagine why on earth Oliver Ferguson wanted to get back in touch after all these years, she said when asked, echoing what her husband had said earlier. 'Unless it's something to do with how easy it is nowadays with social media. People reach middle age like us and start thinking back over the years, wondering about their old school chums. Next thing you know, they're stalking them.'

'That'll be it, darling,' her husband agreed, nodding vigorously.

'Do you mind if I use your loo?' Sal had always prided herself on having a bladder the size of an ox. But these days she couldn't seem to go half an hour without wanting to relieve herself. She blamed that magazine article she'd read in the dentist's waiting room the other week, about keeping oneself hydrated. Now she was never without a bottle of water. She might have noticed a difference in the smoothness of her skin and the fullness of her hair, but it definitely had it downside.

She didn't notice the picture on the way upstairs as she was in so much of a hurry. But she took the journey down at a more leisurely pace. It was a small painting of a house surrounded by trees, no bigger than twenty centimetres by twenty. The colours were dark; and even Sal, who knew nothing about art, sensed a deep gloom emanating from the canvas she couldn't help but find slightly disturbing. It was painted in oils, and the trees were just beginning to shed their leaves. The artist's signature said Tamara Elegant. There was no title, but she didn't need a title to know that she was looking at a picture of Dovecoats.

Sal began to feel that tingle in her tummy she always got when she knew she was onto something. These three friends may well have lost touch over the years, but they'd been close enough once. Maybe even to share a house together.

★   ★   ★

When DC Paddy Bradshaw turned up at the office where Oscar Ferguson worked, he quickly found out that Ferguson hadn't turned up that morning. He should have followed his instincts and simply enquired by phone before making the journey.

But no. Her Ladyship wanted Ferguson to know that they were after him, she'd said. So he'd been the one to draw the short straw that had put him on the motorway slap bang in the middle of the rush hour. And now, by the look of things, it had all been to no avail.

He'd just back in the car and turned it round to drive back down the M11 to Strapley, where he'd hoped to avail himself of a bacon sandwich at the service station, when the message had come through from Keris Brewster that she'd had a call from Ferguson's missus. Apparently her husband had been in accident, she'd said; and since she'd just this morning been made aware that the police were anxious to talk to him, she thought it would be in the public interest if she divulged the name of the hospital where he might be found.

'She's all heart, this one,' Keris said when she'd passed on the news.

'Yes, well, that's what marriage does to you,' Paddy had replied, as one who knew.

It had been another wild goose chase. Two hours later, when he'd arrived at the hospital where Ferguson was meant to be, he learned that he'd discharged himself, despite being advised that he really ought to stay where he was till they could be one hundred per cent sure that he was fit to leave.

'If you do find him,' one of the orderlies said as Paddy was about to go, 'you might want to give him his phone back. It's in two pieces, but I'm sure your techies will be able to put it together again. And who knows what they might find.'

He'd no sooner got back to the station — depositing the phone with the techies and making sure they knew it was *him* they should get back to if they came across anything interesting on his phone, and not anyone else in the investigation team — than he stumbled across Keris Brewster.

'Found anything useful?' she asked him, bright-eyed and bushy-tailed as usual.

'Nothing,' he said. 'Looks like he's done a runner. I've just put a call out for uniform to keep their eyes peeled.'

He hadn't exactly, but that was his plan. Once he'd got himself some breakfast. Though by now it was nearer lunchtime. He suspected Brewster was sniffing around for a bit more info, but she could sniff all she wanted. He had no intention of even mentioning the smart phone or where it was now until he'd got something interesting back from the guys. Otherwise she'd be round there worming information out of them and stealing his glory in no time. This was going to be all his, thank you very much. He needed something to prove to the super that he was just as capable as Sal Jones and that he never should have been passed over for the job she'd snatched from his hands in the first place.

When her phone rang, she picked it up immediately. He heard her say 'Yes it is' and then she went quiet, like what she was listening to was really important and she didn't want to put the person off at the other end in case they rang off and never got back in touch again. When she finished the call, she looked like the cat that'd got the cream, fist pumping the air enthusiastically.

'So, what you got?' It was a struggle not to sound too enthusiastic.

'That was someone called Jade Robinson,' she said, hardly able to contain herself. 'And she's just identified our body at Dovecoats. He's called Darren Openshaw. They were in care together.'

'That's something,' Paddy Bradshaw said grudgingly.

'It's more than something,' Keris replied. 'He wrote to her from Dovecoats back in August 1985. She has the letter he sent still. And what's more, she's coming in with it, right now.'

★   ★   ★

Paddy Bradshaw might not have looked busy, but appearances could be deceptive. 'I'm expecting a call,' he said to Keris Brewster, who was eyeing him accusingly from over by the kettle, a chocolate digestive halfway to her mouth. She was obviously one of those women who couldn't bear the sight of a man looking idle, he decided. He pitied her boyfriend, if she had one. He imagined her shoving a duster in the poor bloke's hand just because he'd committed the crime of sitting down with the remote control and a beer for five minutes.

Ever since she'd had that call from Jade

Robinson, she'd done nothing but pace the room and eat biscuits. How she managed to keep so skinny, he had no idea. Of course it would catch up with her once she hit her thirties, all that snacking. It invariably did. Take his ex. The skinny lass he'd married at the age of twenty-five was four stone heavier by the time they'd got divorced ten years later.

'Can I just say something?' Keris suddenly piped up.

'Be my guest,' Paddy replied.

Keris took a deep breath then came right out with it. 'Do you think you could stop cracking your knuckles?'

Paddy glanced up at her from his desk, surprised. Cracking his knuckles? What on earth was she talking about? He'd been doing nothing of the sort. He racked his brains for something to say by way of a retort, but suddenly the door burst open to reveal one of the techies he'd spoken to earlier, a lad who looked about fifteen with a face full of spots, and trousers halfway down his backside. When he spoke, his face shiny with enthusiasm and pubescent oil slicks, he addressed both of them. This was not what had been agreed at all. Paddy could have thumped him.

'I've been all over that phone you gave me,' said the intruder. 'A woman called Ally's left several messages on it over the last few days.'

'What's this?' Keris wandered over to the techie, who was holding a laptop in front of him like it was surgically attached to his wrists. It probably was, come to think of it. These computer whizz kids lived their lives in virtual reality. To them, being out of reach of a device was worse than being starved of oxygen.

'I said, what's this, Paddy?' she repeated.

'I was going to tell you,' he insisted. 'But then you got the call from whatsername. I managed to get hold of Oscar Ferguson's broken phone from the hospital, that's all.'

Her sharp eyes flickered over his face contemptuously, then slid away. Everything else she said she addressed solely to the techie. It was like Paddy had suddenly become invisible.

'Nick, isn't it?' she said, simpering at him.

'That's right,' the boy simpered back, blushing to the roots of his gelled hair.

'Lovely,' she said. 'Now what is it you heard on that phone?'

'A message,' he said, beaming like the sun at sunset. 'Would you like to hear it?'

'I most certainly would,' she replied, all sweetness and light.

⋆ ⋆ ⋆

'Now, tell me about this picture.'

Sal laid it flat on the only bit of kitchen worktop that wasn't covered in dirty crocks. By the look of things, conversation had stalled in her absence. It was like everyone was just standing around, waiting for her to come back. Well, she was here now. Frazer strolled over to take a look, picking up the picture and studying it at close range before gently putting it back down again.

'I'm guessing you two already know what it's a picture of,' Sal said. 'But in case you don't, I'll describe it to you.'

156

Tamara and Henry stood stiffly side by side, not touching, while Sal spoke. When one of Tamara's arms accidentally brushed her husband's jacket, she pulled it away immediately like she'd just got an electric shock. Or like the thought of actually touching her husband repelled her. What sort of marriage was this? Sal wondered.

She'd felt queasy ever since the super had brought up the subject of putting her in front of a camera, and the smell of last night's dinner wafting up off all those dirty dishes was making things worse. On top of that, it was beginning to get hot in the room, and she was beginning to find it hard to concentrate.

What Sal really wanted was a sit-down. But she suspected the Morrish-Elegants were already looking down on her, albeit metaphorically, just for being a mere police officer and not something more creative like an artist or someone in advertising. Sitting down would just make her look smaller.

'Earlier on, Mr Morrish, you said you'd lost touch with Oscar Ferguson when you both left school. And that your wife barely even knew him. Yet here's this lovely picture of his godmother's house. And with your signature on it too, Tamara.'

Sal recognised panic in Tamara Elegant's eyes. In an attempt to cover it up, she gabbled her next words. But it was a stupid ploy. All it did was amplify it.

'You took me there once, remember, Hal?' she said, tossing back her hair. 'I think you were trying to encourage me to get on a bit better with your best friend. I suppose he must have been staying there with his godmother. It didn't work out, though. I never really warmed to him. Though *she* was charming.' She gave a little tinkle of a laugh, fixing her husband with a smile that stopped at her eyes.

'Oh yes,' he said, nodding his head so vigorously Sal thought it might fall off. 'I think I remember that. You painted it from memory, didn't you? Some time later, as I recall.'

Sal didn't believe a word of it. She got as far as opening her mouth and making an attempt to say so too. But the words seemed to thicken, and got stuck there. The air in the room had turned sticky and hot. She felt it pressing on her from all sides; there was a ringing in her ears and her vision began to blur.

She felt herself begin to slide down the kitchen cabinet she'd been leaning against, and though she wondered about doing something to stop herself from sliding any further, she couldn't. From a long way away, the sound of people's concern floated towards her. 'Oh God, she's fainting,' someone said. Another person squealed. Someone else said, 'Ma'am. I've got you.' Really, such a lot of fuss about nothing.

★   ★   ★

'Honestly, there's absolutely no need for any of this. I'm perfectly OK.'

They were back at the station now, having left the Morrish-Elegants in rather a hurry. Sal had wanted to stay and get to the bottom of the pack of lies she suspected they'd just been told. But Frazer wasn't having it. He practically dragged her out of the kitchen, leaving Henry Morrish and his wife staring open-mouthed behind them, very likely unable to believe their luck at having got away with it.

In the car, he told her that leaving them to stew for a while would make it easier next time. It would give them the chance to weave a whole web of lies between them, and the more intricate the web the easier it would be to blow it apart. And there was Sal thinking he was whisking her back to the station for the good of her health!

Paddy was taking the opportunity of this little chink in the boss's armour to take centre stage, brandishing the information that Nick the techie had uncovered with great aplomb.

'I've sent him off to find out from the phone data who this Ally is,' he ended by saying. 'Once we've got a name and address, we can bring her in.'

'Excellent,' Sal said. 'She can tell us who her friend Ruth is too. They're obviously all in it together.'

She was beginning to regret her failure

to overrule Frazer by bringing in the Morrish-Elegants, since it was blindingly obvious that 'Henry and that girlfriend of his' were the very people Ally had referred to at the end of her message.

'Any more news on Oscar?' she wanted to know.

Paddy shook his head. 'Nada.'

But just then, a uniformed officer stuck his head round the door. 'Your man Oscar's in custody down at Walthamstow nick,' he announced. 'Seems he got into a fight with an ATM.'

Paddy jumped up. 'Let me do this,' he said. 'I've been chasing that slippery beggar all day.'

Sal had no intention of objecting. From the corner of her eye, she could see Keris fiddling with the coffee machine. She needed to intercept her before she found herself in possession of a beverage she really didn't fancy drinking.

'I'll come with you.' Frazer leaped up from his seat and followed Paddy to the door.

'What about Jade Robinson?' Keris called out after them. 'Don't you want to know about her?'

Sal and Frazer, who was halfway out of the door by now, exchanged perplexed expressions. Jade who?

It looked like they'd been having far more success at this end than Frazer and her, Sal thought. Not only had they failed to catch up with Ferguson at his home, but they'd abandoned an interview with his two accomplices halfway through. Suppose, when they went back to finish off what they'd started, the couple had skipped it, taking their family with them? Oh God, it was just too much to even contemplate.

'I'll fill you in en route, Frazer,' Paddy said. 'Keris'll tell you all about it too, ma'am, I'm sure.'

The two of them shot off at speed, forgetting to close the door behind them, naturally, so a draught whistled through. Sal strode over to the door to shut it for them. The two men were halfway down the corridor by now, but Paddy Bradshaw had a loud voice and it carried.

'She don't look too good, does she?' she heard him say. 'Wouldn't be surprised if the super's beginning to wonder if he's done the right thing, taking on a menopausal woman for a job like this.'

Menopausal! She'd give him menopausal. She had at least ten years to go before that kicked in. 'There's nothing wrong with my hearing, Bradshaw,' she muttered, slamming the door with force. When she turned round, Keris was tipping coffee beans into the grinder. 'I'll pass on that, Keris,' she said. 'I'd rather have a cup of tea, if that's all right. Coffee can make me feel a bit queasy if I have too much in one day.' Actually, she'd not had any today. But she liked Keris and she didn't want to hurt her feelings. 'Tell me about this Jade Robinson, then,' she said.

'Queasy?' Keris, still clutching the grinder, observed her, a wry smile on her face. 'That brings back memories.'

'How do you mean?'

'Well, there's sixteen years between me and my little sister. My mum and dad divorced, and our Susie and me have different fathers.'

Back into the cupboard went the coffee

grinder, and out came the tea caddy. Where was this leading? Sal wondered.

'So I remember everything about my mum's pregnancy?'

'You what?'

'Yeah. Coffee was the first thing she went off. And she'd been dreadful for the stuff till then.'

Sal swallowed hard. Her heart started banging like a drum.

'Coffee, then wine,' Keris went on. 'Just the smell of it made her feel ill.'

Wine? What had she said to Jeff last night when he'd poured her that glass of Chardonnay? There's something wrong with this, that's what she'd said. He'd sniffed it and sniffed it again. Then he'd told her if she didn't want it he'd drink it, which he promptly did, of course.

'Are you all right, boss?'

'Yes,' Sal said, struggling to keep the hysteria out of her voice. 'Yes, I am.'

She needed to pull herself together. First minute she got to herself, she'd be down at the chemist's. But for now she had a job to do.

'I'm still waiting to find out who this

Jade Robinson is,' she said. 'And hurry up with that tea, will you, Keris, before I die of thirst.'

* * *

If every line on a person's face told a story, then Jade Robinson must have led some life. She sat opposite them in the soft interview room, pulling her cheap leopard-skin coat around her skinny frame. Each time she leaned across the table to make a point, she gave off a whiff of cheap perfume and cigarette smoke.

The letter, scrawled in green ink on badly creased writing paper yellowed with age, lay in the space between them, Sal and Keris on one side of the table and Jade on the other. It was brief and, Sal couldn't help think, oddly moving.

'Dear Jade,' it began. 'Sorry for the writing only they hadent got any proper paper with lines only this plane stuff so it's a bit of a mess.'

He wasn't wrong there. His sentences crawled all over the page, in search of the right direction but never finding it.

'Sorry I havent been in touch before too but you no me and riting,' the letter went on. 'Am staying in this big house called Duvcoats in a place called Lampliegh. Don't ask me how I got here.

'Anyway there is no need for you to worry about me becos I landed on my feet with these posh kids. 5 of them tho 2 is just kids really. But lots of food, booze and weed. And they sed I can stay till the end of the sumer when Oscars good muther comes back from her holyday. Hope you are well and bhayving yourself,
    Yours Darren.'

'No kisses, I bet you noticed,' Jade said. She spoke the words glibly, like she'd convinced herself the cops had already made up their minds that she was a mug so she was determined to get in first when it came to the put-downs.

'Tell me about Darren,' Sal said, refusing to acknowledge Jade's remark.

'We grew up together in care,' she said. 'Arrived on the same day at the kids' home. You know what it's like in them places. You've got to make a friend quick. Self-preservation, know what I mean?'

166

Sal could imagine.

'We stuck up for each other,' Jade went on. 'I picked the right one, as it happens. Nothing happened to me when Darren was around.'

'The protective sort?' Keris asked.

Jade raised her over-tweezered brows.

'Crazy more like. Sort that used his fists first *then* asked questions.' She leaned lowered her voice. 'Speaking confidentially, Darren was never out of trouble. Got arrested a few times. Spent some time inside, too.'

They already knew that. Uniform had brought up a long record of offences, ranging from twocking to breaking and entering. Then there was the two-year stretch for assaulting a police officer so badly it put him in hospital for six months. What was the story there, Sal wondered. She was about to find out.

'He wanted to join the army,' Jade said.' For a whole year he was as good as gold. Didn't put a foot wrong. Gave up the fags and the booze. Went running every day. The day they turned him down he went on a bender, badly assaulted a police officer and ended up inside.'

So that was that little incident explained, then.

'He wasn't a bad lad, you know, Officer,' Jade said. 'It was just, well, he didn't know when to rein himself in, do you know what I'm saying? And he wasn't very bright. I'm sure he had that wotsit too. ADDH, is that what it's called?'

It was near enough right. By now Sal had formed a very clear picture of the kind of boy Darren Openshaw had been. What she needed to know now were the circumstances in which he'd stumbled upon Oscar and his little gang.

Five people, so the letter said. Ferguson, Henry Morrish and Tamara Elegant were all more or less of an age. So the 'two kids' would have been Ally and the as yet not fully identified Ruth. Ally Ferguson had been quickly identified as Oscar's younger sister from her phone records. She would have been sixteen in the summer of '85. If she were to hazard a guess, Ruth would have been a school friend.

'What did you do when you got that letter, Jade?' Keris, who so far had been busy writing notes, asked.

'I went to find him,' she said. 'To tell him that he was about to become a father, and what did he intend doing about it?'

'You were pregnant with his child?' Keris said.

'I know. Stupid. But that was me. We'd lost touch once we left the children's home. But then we met up again some years later, by chance.' It was in a pub, she said. She was getting over a relationship, and Darren just happened to walk into the pub where she was drinking to forget it. 'It was a drunken fumble that went too far,' she said rather eloquently, Sal thought.

'When did it happen, this . . . ' Sal paused to give herself time to choose her next word carefully. She settled on 'reunion'.

'A few months before he sent me that letter.'

Getting the letter, when she guessed she must already be at least three months

169

gone, gave her the idea to go after Darren.

'I thought that by giving me his address it was his way of saying he wanted me to come down.' She gave a hollow laugh. 'I know now it was more likely to have been something he let slip by accident. Like I said, he wasn't very bright.'

'So you paid him a visit?'

'Well, that was the idea,' Jade said. 'Except when I got there and knocked on the door, the guy that answered said they had no idea who Darren was. Said he must have made it all up. So I left.'

'Did the guy give his name?'

'I don't remember. It was a long time ago. But he was posh. And he said it was his house till his godmother came back. So it had to be what Darren wrote there, doesn't it?' She stabbed the letter with a red fingernail. 'Oscar.'

There was a sharp rap on the door. When Sal looked up, Frazer was beckoning to her. 'Excuse me a sec,' she said, getting up from her seat but not without picking up Darren's letter to Jade. Frazer needed to see this. Paddy too. They should get copies. 'What is it, Frazer?' she asked him, her hand on the handle of the door.

'You'll love this,' he said. 'We've rounded them all up and they're all on their way here. The Elegant-Morrishes, Oscar Ferguson, his sister Ally — and get this.' He paused for effect. 'The final one — Ruth Edgely. Headmistress at Morley Grange.'

Sal gave a low whistle. There'd been an article about that particular school in one of the Sunday magazines the other week. It cost a fortune to send your daughter there, and when it came to achievement it was right up there with the best of the boys' public schools, even surpassing many.

It looked like the stage was set for the final act to begin. The actors were waiting in the wings. She couldn't wait.

'How are you feeling now, ma'am by the way?' Frazer asked her.

Sal rubbed her hands together gleefully. 'Do you know,' she said joyfully, 'I've never felt better. There's nothing like the scent of success to get the blood coursing through my veins again, Frazer.'

August 1985

It had all been going so well. He'd had great lifts all the way down from Manchester. Dropped lucky too with the older woman who'd stood him an all-day breakfast in that last motorway café. Unfortunately she wasn't going any further, she'd said. Darren got the idea she was meeting a man who wasn't her husband — there was definitely something about her that made him think she was up to no good.

After they'd parted ways, he found himself hanging about round the petrol pumps, feeling a bit sorry for himself. Not just because it had started raining, though that was bad enough. But at the prospect of having to hitch another lift. Drivers rarely picked up young men on their own anymore. He could be standing there with his thumb out for days before anyone stopped.

Then out of the blue, some bloke in charge of a big freight lorry said, 'Jump in if you're going to London.' Who was he to refuse? Foreign bloke, he was. Said he was from Poland. To break the ice, Darren told him his sister was married to a Polish bloke. It was all a pack of lies, of course. He didn't even have a sister. But if he did, she'd have been called Janine, her Polish husband would have been called Lukas after that footballer he'd heard about who'd scored the fastest goal in history, and their two kids would have been called Darren after himself and Mary after his mother. Which was another lie, because his mother was called Maureen. Not that he remembered her much. The bits he did remember he wished he could forget.

When he got out his gear to roll himself a joint, he assumed Peter — because they were on first-name terms by now — would be cool with it. It came as a bit of a shock when he pulled up in the next lay-by and told him to get out. He was a big bloke, and mad as hell, so Darren wasn't going to argue with him.

A two-mile trek in the drizzle of an English summer brought him to the outskirts of a village. It took him no time to work out that Lampleigh was the type of place rich people would live in. People who were out at work all day making lots of lovely dosh and who left their houses empty.

But people who made lots of money weren't stupid. He could see the alarms from the road. Some places looked like they might even have CCTV. He was low on funds but it wasn't worth the risk.

Then he found himself standing outside a big old rambling house where no matter how hard he looked, there was no sign of an alarm. What harm would it do just to have a little wander inside and a look-see?

He wished Jade was here. She'd give him a proper talking-to if she could see him being tempted like this. 'You don't have to steal, Daz,' she was always telling him when they were younger.

He hadn't got back in touch after that one night. He would have liked to, but it was obvious she was still pining for some other guy, and you could say what you liked about him but he did have some pride. Maybe down the line sometime he'd get back in touch, pay her another visit, see if she'd straightened herself out.

The gate to the big house was off its latch. He pushed it open and wandered inside. The garden was overgrown and the lawn looked like it had been a while since it had had a shave. He used to like gardening when he was a kid in the home. Mrs Jenkins used to tell him he had green fingers. From the look of the place, whoever lived here could use a gardener. Probably some little old lady, too frail to take care of it on her own these days.

In his head he practised the words. Imagined speaking them to his imaginary old lady, who'd take an instant shine to him.

'You don't know anybody who needs a gardener or an odd job man, do you?' he'd say.

It was a bit of a surprise when he finally got round to plucking up courage enough to actually knock on the door, to discover that the person who opened it wasn't an old lady but a guy his own age. And from the look of him, he was pretty stoned.

Keris was flattered. She liked to think that Sal had asked her to interview Ruth Edgely because Edgely was a tough nut and it required another tough nut to crack her. Sal couldn't do it herself, since she'd had to 'pop out' somewhere. She hadn't said where, but Keris hadn't got to the rank of detective constable at the age of twenty-five without being able to put two and two together. When she'd brought up the subject of her mum's pregnancy symptoms, she saw the look on Sal's face. It was like all of a sudden the penny had dropped. Without a doubt, her boss had nipped to the precinct to pick up a pregnancy test.

'Now, Ms Edgely,' Keris began, 'I appreciate that you're a very busy woman. But this is a serious investigation. We have reason to believe that Darren Openshaw was either murdered or involved in an accident that led to his death in the summer of 1985. Certain phone records would suggest that you were present at the time of this man's death.'

Ruth Edgely glared at Keris through her very expensive wing-tipped spectacles. She did rather excel in those headmistressy glares, there was no denying it. Keris wondered if you had to take an exam in them before you could qualify to be in charge of your own school.

'Look here! If I'm being accused of something, then I'm saying nothing until I've called my solicitor.'

Oh God, not another one. Before she'd set foot in the interview room, Keris had had a little confab with Frazer and a more than usually miserable Paddy. Frazer had informed her that Oscar and his sister Ally were also demanding solicitors. Unfortunately they shared the same one — a family friend apparently — and Oscar had insisted on having first dibs on him.

Right now, Ally was sitting in one of the waiting rooms with a uniformed police constable for company, twiddling her thumbs, no doubt working out her story, while she waited for her brother's interview to come to an end.

Henry Morrish and Tamara Elegant, interviewed separately in the presence of duty solicitors, had both answered 'no comment' to every single question Paddy had put before them, which was the reason for his present mood.

'I'm not accusing you of anything, Ruth,' Keris said. 'I just want to know about that summer. The summer of 1985. You were there at Dovecoats, with Oscar and Ally Ferguson, Henry Morrish and Tamara Elegant, weren't you?'

'Yes. Yes I was. Ally was my best friend from school. Oscar was her older brother. She asked me along for company because the others — this Henry and his girlfriend — were much older than us.'

Two years older, that was all. But when you were sixteen, even a gap of six months in either direction was huge.

'And did you meet Darren Openshaw?'

Ruth shrugged. 'Yes. He was creepy, eyeing Ally and me up and down all the time. Ally's godmother had this amazing library, and I spent most of my time in there. It was the best place to hide from him. Not to mention the booze and the drugs and all the other carrying on.'

'There was a lot of that, was there? Carrying on?'

Ruth blushed. 'Don't ask me to go into details,' she said. 'They were a bunch of kids let loose for the first time for the whole summer. I'm sure you can imagine.'

Keris could. She'd been a teenager herself once, though these days it seemed a very long time ago.

'The place stank of dope. And nobody did any washing up or cleaning.' Ruth Edgely tossed her beautifully cut bob disdainfully. 'I'd led a very sheltered life till then, Detective,' she said. 'Things were different at Dovecoats. It was anarchy, frankly; and after I'd been there three weeks, I told Ally I'd had enough and I was going to ring my mother to come and get me.'

In the end, she hadn't, she said. Ally had been frightened that if her mother had seen the state of the house, she'd have contacted Ally's mother and then she'd have been made to leave too. In the end, she'd persuaded her brother to drive

Ruth to the nearest station and put her on a train without getting any of the parents involved.

'So Ally was quite happy to stay, then?'

'Oh, she was lapping up all the attention from Darren,' Ruth said bitterly. 'It was at Dovecoats where she discovered she had a taste for booze and cannabis, you know. One short summer to get hooked. The next fifteen years to get off the stuff.'

Her brother and his friends had been totally irresponsible, she said. Ally had just been a child.

'I can't tell you how much I regret not doing more to get her away from that house,' she continued. 'She may have got off the drugs and the alcohol, but she's never really got her life back together. She even spent some time in a mental health unit. It's as if that summer blighted her whole life.'

'What could you have done, though? She sounds like a very willful girl.'

'I could have told my mother what was going on and she'd have done something. But instead I walked away, relieved to see

180

the back of the place.'

A wistful expression crossed her face. It was like she was back there again, an adolescent girl powerless to stop the tide of her friend's reckless behaviour. But then it changed, replaced by her determined-headmistress face. 'But believe me,' she said, 'nowadays, if I notice something — even the smallest thing — that gives me cause for concern in any of my pupil's well-being, I make it my business to intervene right away.'

Well, we can draw a line through this one's name, Keris decided. If she was a stick of rock and you cut her open, you'd find the word 'integrity' running right through her. But something Ruth had said kept twanging on Keris's brain. She knew it had to be significant. She just didn't know how yet.

It's as if that whole summer blighted her whole life, she'd said. What would do that? she wondered. Could *she* have murdered Darren Openshaw? You'd need to be strong to do that; and anyway, if what Ruth said was true, she'd developed a bit of a crush on him.

But what if she'd witnessed a murder committed by someone she loved? Olly, for instance. She'd been desperate to avoid getting him into trouble with her parents and had gone to great lengths to find another way to get him off the premises without involving her mother. How much further would she go to keep her beloved older brother out of trouble?

★   ★   ★

Oscar Ferguson looked like a man who'd been put through the wringer several times. Nothing like that Facebook photo Frazer had caught a glimpse of on his laptop yesterday, when they'd paid him a visit at home hoping to catch him there.

'Why did you tell Jade Robinson that you had no idea who Darren Openshaw was?'

Frazer had been accommodating up till this point, enduring the interminable silences after each question he'd asked while Ferguson checked with his solicitor whether or not he should answer. It'd taken them the best part of fifteen minutes to prise his name and address out of him and establish that during the summer of 1985 he'd been looking after Dovecoats for his godmother, Miss Eleanor Godley, and unbeknown to her had invited some of his friends to stay.

'You know, we were pretty high most of the time,' Oscar said. 'Could be I was just too out of it when she turned up.'

He really was a rotten liar. Frazer slid Jade's letter across the table toward him. 'That's your name written down there,' he said. 'One of the few words he managed to spell correctly.'

Oscar peered at the wavy green ink for a long time. Then, after he'd spent ages fumbling for his glasses in his jacket pocket, he said he didn't have his glasses with him.

'I'll save you the time, shall I?' Frazer said, and read it out loud. 'Come on, now, Oscar,' he added, when he'd put the letter down. 'You were there. He was there. His body — no, his skeleton — turns up in the grounds wrapped in an old rug some thirty-five years later. You get in touch with the very same friend who was there with you. You get a ton of messages from your sister.' He steepled his hands, his elbows resting on the table. 'You've got to see it from where I'm sitting, Oscar. You're in this up to your neck.'

'I didn't do it.'

He really looked like he was about to burst into tears. The solicitor glared at Frazer, who put up his hands in a gesture of surrender.

'Fine,' he said. 'Good. We're getting there at last. So if you didn't do it, then tell me who did.'

'I can't,' he said. 'I made a promise.'

★   ★   ★

Palmer's Court was her last home, and the artificial lake would be her final resting place. It had been easy to persuade Layla, her favourite helper, to wheel her down to this spot at dusk.

The old and the ancient were indulged here; that was what they paid thousands a month for. All it took was some sentimental story about how at her age

184

one never knew how many more dusks one would see. She'd sent the girl back to get her binoculars, which she said she'd forgotten, insisting it would only take her five minutes tops to locate them.

'What harm could I possibly come to, wrapped up in my furs, safe in my bath chair?' she'd exclaimed. *And my pockets full of stones*, she'd failed to add. Layla would never find them, since they were right here in her handbag. But the girl was nothing if not thorough. Eleanor knew her well enough to predict that she would turn her suite upside down before hurrying back to tell her they were nowhere to be found. By then, of course, it would be too late.

Eleanor closed her eyes and willed herself back in time. She'd been so successful at shutting down that part of her memory over the years that it took a great deal of effort to summon up the events of that night. She'd returned from holiday a week early — hadn't thought to tell Oscar she was coming, too distraught at the way her summer idyll had ended to think about anyone but herself.

At the start of that summer she'd been a middle-aged woman grown young again through love. Admittedly with a married man. But a married man besotted with her enough to abandon his wife and family and go with her to Europe, where they'd spent the summer together. But after a few weeks it had all gone horribly wrong. She'd tried to ignore the warning signs at first — the distracted look on his face as she tried to engage him in conversation; the furtive manner in which he put down the phone whenever she came into the room.

The evening she'd overheard him telling his wife that he'd made a mistake, and if she'd have him back he was coming home, had sent Eleanor rushing to her room to pack. She'd always been a proud woman. She would not wait around to hear Charles tell her that their affair was over. Less than three hours later she was on a flight home.

The nearer she got to home, the more furious she grew. Her contempt for Charles threatened to swallow her up. She couldn't stop thinking about the relief in his eyes when she'd told him she was leaving and the ease with which he'd said goodbye.

By the time the cab drew up in the middle of the night outside Dovecoats, she was incensed with anger, jumpy with nerves, at war with the entire world. She'd let herself in and strode immediately into the drawing room to find a drink.

At first she didn't notice them. She was far more concerned with the state of the room. She'd trusted that boy to keep an eye on the place and he'd turned it into a pigsty. Indignantly, she picked up the heavy brass lamp that someone had so carelessly overturned. She would give that boy a piece of her mind come the morning.

But then she thought she heard someone sigh, someone else breathe softly. Surely she wasn't imagining it — the sound of bodies shifting? Still with the lamp in her hand, she strode over to switch on the main light. Immediately the room was flooded with brightness.

What happened next was over so

quickly that she sometimes wondered if she'd dreamed it. Ally, why — she was a just a child! Naked, wrapped in the arms of some man, similarly unclothed.

'Get off my goddaughter immediately and get out of my house before I call the police,' she screamed.

She hadn't given him any time at all. He was half on and half off the settee when she'd brought the lamp down on his head. Once. Twice. Three times. Each time Ally's screams grew louder until the whole house was summoned by her noise.

There they stood. Olly, blinking himself awake. His two friends, a boy and girl she vaguely remembered being introduced to once, clinging onto to each other, afraid to look but unable to turn their eyes away from the grisly scene. And throughout, the sound of Ally's crazy keening.

Eleanor removed the letter she'd written from her bag and laid it on the grass for someone to find and give to the police. Then she let the brake off the chair and rolled herself towards the water.

It was not their fault. None of it was their fault. The letter would explain that.

They'd done it for her, because they were afraid and in shock. The two boys had rolled him up and buried him below ground. She'd made them promise not to speak of it, and all this time they hadn't. Well, now they would be able to.

* * *

Sal folded the letter and returned it to the envelope. Another case resolved. All she could think was, how could someone keep a secret for so long? None of them had been able to explain fully. They were kids, young and frightened. Eleanor Godley was a grown-up. She'd told them Darren Openshaw was scum. He'd taken advantage of a much younger girl. Made Ally say he'd forced her. They'd wrecked her house and taken advantage of her hospitality. Broken things and ruined the carpets. Done the sort of stuff that made your parents livid. If she kept their secret, then they'd keep hers.

Sal patted the jacket pocket where the pregnancy test nestled. She had a secret of her own at the moment — although she suspected Keris had cottoned on to it even before she had herself. Of course, she could have done the test here, in the ladies' loo at the office. But she wanted to share the moment with Jeff. Some secrets were better shared.

A NOVEL WAY TO DIE

Kim couldn't wait to get inside the house and into the warm. The day had been a cold, damp one and all she'd done with it was chase after villains who didn't want to be caught. Now she was tired. This morning, as she'd rolled out of bed at the hour of Unearthly, Michael had reminded her that it was his turn to cook tonight. She couldn't wait to get stuck in to a plateful of the chilli con carne he'd promised.

Funny, but there was no light coming from inside. Kim found her key and let herself in by the light of the street lamp. Something else struck her as odd. An absence of cooking smells matched by an eerie silence.

'Michael?'

No reply. As she took a step forward, her regulation boot struck something solid. She swore under her breath as she fumbled for the light switch. In the middle of the hallway, blocking her route to the kitchen, stood a big cardboard box full of books. There must have been at least forty of them, every one identical, with the title *A Person of Interest* picked out in embossed gold print above the name of the author, Storm Costello, and a typically moody black-and-white cover of a rugged-looking man in an overcoat, smoking a cigarette and leaning on his car.

It took a while before she recalled where she'd seen the name before. Then she remembered Storm Costello was the crime writer Michael had booked to do a Q&A the following week. Couldn't he have had the damn books delivered to the library instead of to the house? He was the chief librarian. Surely that entitled you to some perks?

Kim groped in her jacket pocket for her phone. Damn! Two missed calls from Michael, both before ten this morning, and two messages. Worse, a voicemail from Shannon. Voicemails from Shannon usually went on forever and rarely boded well. In fact, nothing that involved her sister was ever less than complicated. Kim decided to deal with Michael first. At least she could guarantee he'd be coherent.

Such an idiot, read his first message. Got the date wrong. SC coming tonight. Won't be around to cook after all. Apologies. Hope you can come along. Need all the support I can get.

Kim swore again, but out loud this time. The last thing she wanted was to go out again. Particularly if it involved playing hostess to an author whose books she was going to have to admit she'd never even read.

She hadn't wanted to say anything to Michael, but only the previous week she'd read a couple of reviews of Storm Costello's latest novel, knowing she'd be visiting the library to talk to an audience of her fans about it. The consensus appeared to be that her heroine was a bit of a drip and that there were far too many coincidences to make the plot believable.

Worse, one of the reviews even suggested that the new book was almost a retelling of *Dead Giveaway*, her third novel and the one she'd first made her name with. If anyone who'd been thinking about going along to Orton Library tonight had, like Kim, read these reviews, they might very well have decided an evening in front of the telly was a much better option.

But then she thought of poor Michael stuck on his tod with just the author and an audience of two. If the boot were on the other foot, he wouldn't think twice of coming to her rescue. And as soon as she read his second message, sent less than an hour ago when she'd been driving home with the car radio blaring, she knew she had no choice.

Mental here, he'd written. *Sheila can't stay. Sick dog. Plus completely forgot books. No time to come home & pick up. Do you think you could help me out and bring them here?*

So that was that, then. Her night sorted out for her. If Sheila, Michael's competent assistant, wasn't there, then he'd be floundering. A sensible person would have ignored Shannon's message, having concluded that what you didn't know couldn't hurt you. But Kim was a great believer in facing life's obstacles all at once. That way you knew what you'd got. And as far as obstacles went, she could always rely on her sister.

'Kim. It's Dad,' Shannon's voicemail went. 'You're not going to believe this. He's got a girlfriend. I spotted them from the bus window this afternoon while I was on my way to work. I don't know about you, but I'm not happy about this.'

No, you wouldn't be, Kim thought. Shannon was rarely happy at the thought of anyone finding contentment. She'd absolutely loved it when Kim had put her life on hold and moved in with Dad to help him get back on his feet after Mum's death. But then she'd gone and spoiled it all for Shannon by meeting Michael and finding happiness.

'You'll have to go round and talk to him. Sooner the better. Tonight, when you come off shift. I'd go myself, only I've got the girls,' she continued.

Ah yes, the girls. Lily and Mandy. Shannon's permanently extenuating circumstances. If Dad *had* met somebody else, then more power to him, Kim mused. After mum had died, he'd put his life on hold for a good eighteen months. But gradually he'd begun to embrace a social life again. These days he had a busier one than she did, what with U3A and the bowls and his French conversation class. Where had he met this new woman? she wondered. Wherever it had been, she had no intention of barging round there at this time of night sticking her oar in where it wasn't wanted. Let Shannon stew. With one swipe of her finger, she deleted her voicemail before replying to Michael's text.

With you soon with books, she wrote.

Look on the bright side, she told herself as she struggled to lift the box that contained them. She'd be back home in two and a half hours, tops. Then she'd be able to put this day behind her for good.

★ ★ ★

It was gone seven thirty by the time Kim drew up outside the library with the box of books in tow. Michael came hurrying out to meet her, looking even more anxious and dishevelled than he normally did at these events. She longed to get a comb to his hair and straighten his tie. But clearly now was not the right time.

'What's up?' she said, unsnapping her seat belt and hopping out of the car. 'Got the wine order wrong? Do you need me to go and get more supplies?'

Michael shook his head as Kim made her way round to the back of the car and went to open the boot.

'Voilà,' she said, making a sweeping gesture with her arm.

He gave her a look of gratitude. It had nearly killed her lifting that box into the boot. But he removed it with remarkable ease for a man who never worked out and spent most of his days crouched over a computer.

'So what's bothering you, then?' she asked him.

He strode briskly towards the library entrance, carrying the heavy load as if it were a box of bubble wrap. 'Am I so transparent?' he said.

'No, not really.' She paused, then

added, 'Well, yes, actually, I suppose you are.'

'She's late,' he said just as the entrance door slid open to admit them. 'And I'm worried.'

Kim pretended she hadn't heard. She'd kept her side of the bargain, lugging that box here and giving herself a bad case of lumbago into the bargain. She wasn't going to allow herself to become infected by Michael's obsessive timekeeping.

As they entered, heads turned towards them expectantly, and the chatter died down. There was quite a crowd present, mostly women of a certain age, and mostly all clutching a glass. Suddenly finding all eyes on her, Kim felt distinctly uncomfortable.

'Very nice,' she whispered. 'I like how you've done the chairs. And the flowers on the table are a nice touch.'

Michael ignored her remark. 'I mean late, late,' he hissed through the side of his mouth. 'She was due fifteen minutes ago.' He attempted a reassuring smile for the audience. Though it didn't look too reassuring to Kim. He looked like a man about to be sent to the gallows. 'I've tried ringing her but she's not picking up,' he added.

'Look,' she said, forgetting her vow not to get any more involved than she already was, 'you go and entertain them. Give me your phone. I'll try ringing her again.'

'Would you? That would be great.' Michael plonked the box of books down on the nearest table, fumbled in his pocket for his mobile, scrolled down for Storm Costello's number and handed the phone over. 'Let's hope you'll have better luck than me,' he said.

Once outside, Kim tried the number he'd given her. 'Come on,' she murmured as she keyed it in. 'Pick up for me.'

But sadly, all she got was Storm Costello's pleasantly resonant accentless voice inviting her to leave a message. Kim listened till the end but declined to do so, pretty sure Michael would have left at least one already, the state he was in. She was about to go back inside when the phone suddenly started ringing again. Storm's name flashed up on the screen. At last!

'Ms Costello,' Kim began.

She got no further than that. Whoever it was on the other end it wasn't Storm Costello. For a start, it was a man. Second, the accent was all wrong. Third, within moments of him starting to talk, she thought she recognised the voice.

'This PC Alan Togher. Who am I speaking to, please?' the person on the other end said.

Alan? She was right, then. What on earth was Alan doing on Storm Costello's phone? She'd spoken to him only that evening as she was coming off duty and he was coming on.

'It's me, Al,' Kim said. 'Kim. I'm calling on my partner's phone. Storm Costello is meant to be here. At the library. Giving a talk. Remember I told you about it?'

She hesitated to ask him what had happened. When you get a police officer picking up a phone that didn't belong to him, you could be pretty sure he wouldn't be giving you good news. What Alan said next confirmed it.

'There's been an RTA Kim,' he said.

'Lucky you rang when you did. Until then, we didn't have an identity.'

Kim's blood ran cold. 'Identity?' she said. 'Is she dead?'

There was another pause. 'We'll know more when the ambulance gets here.'

'So what happened?'

'From what I can tell, she came off the road and wrapped the car round a tree. Luckily she wasn't going fast.'

At this point, Alan seemed to break up. She thought she heard something about waiting for an ambulance. Then she heard the siren itself. 'Look. I've got to go,' he said.

'Yes,' Kim muttered. 'Yes, of course. You have to work to do.'

And so had she. She had bad news to deliver. Tonight's event was cancelled.

*   *   *

The next morning, Kim was meant to be paying a MOP visit — a visit to a member of the public — to apologise for taking so long to come out and see them about an incident involving some discarded needles

201

outside their house. She figured that since they'd already waited a week, they wouldn't be overly anxious at having to wait a bit longer. In fact, they might well have concluded that the police had forgotten about them altogether.

Michael had called the hospital early to ask after Storm Costello. Of course, they wouldn't tell him anything since he wasn't related to her, so Kim, with her police officer's hat on, had volunteered to have another go.

The patient was doing well, she was told. Fortunately, her injuries were superficial. Michael was interviewing that morning, so Kim suggested she pay her a visit instead of him and pass on his good wishes, along with the bouquet of flowers she suggested he ought to cough up for as a get-well-soon token.

She'd expected a gentle whey-faced lady writer lying in her bed with her leg in plaster and very much out of it. But what she got instead was a woman of robust appearance struggling to get out of bed while arguing with a harassed-looking man who was struggling to put her back in it again.

'Honestly, there's absolutely no need for all this fuss,' Storm Costello complained, throwing off the man's arm.

Kim appeared to have walked straight into a domestic. When the couple realised they weren't alone, the man immediately dropped the woman's arm. Storm Costello straightened her hospital gown as her gaze came to rest on the bunch of flowers.

'Are those for me?' she said, her expression immediately softening.

Kim explained her mission, adding she was glad to see Ms Costello wasn't as badly hurt as everyone at the library event last night, Michael and herself included, had feared.

'As you see,' she said, 'It's just a few cuts and bruises.'

'Don't forget your wonky ankle.'

Storm Costello rolled her eyes and gave a long sigh. 'Dougie darling,' she said, 'take the flowers and ask one of those nice nurses to put them in water, would you?'

Dougie meekly trotted off, leaving Kim alone with the patient, who'd climbed back into bed. Who was he, exactly? Kim wondered. Her minder or her partner?

'I'm not staying in this place any longer than another day,' Storm said, picking up the argument with Kim where she'd left off with Dougie.

'Well, it's not up to me,' Kim said. 'What have the doctors said?'

Storm Costello gave a snort. 'Doctors? What do they know?'

Kim had no idea how to respond to this one.

'Oh dear, what must we look like,' Storm said breezily. 'You mustn't think Dougie and I row like that all the time,' she added, smoothing the bed sheet. 'My husband adores me. He just doesn't understand how much it takes out of me, trying to create a novel.'

Apparently he'd been trying to persuade her to go home with him and not to stick to the plan she'd made before the accident happened.

'Ah yes,' Kim said. 'Owl Cottage. Of course.' She'd read for herself the email Storm had sent asking Michael if he could recommend somewhere she might be able to take a short lease on. Her plan, she'd written, was to head there straight after the library event and to 'hunker down', as she put it, until her novel was complete. Instead of sending her a link to the local letting agency, which had been Kim's suggestion, Michael, always hyper-meticulous, had spent hours faffing about on the internet researching suitable places himself.

'I'm not changing my plans just because of a few scratches.' Storm Costello spoke in a way that challenged anyone to try and stop her doing otherwise. 'I'm at a critical point and there's no way I'll be able to make any progress with it at home.'

Douglas, back from searching for a nurse, happened to choose this moment to overhear her words. *Ding, ding, round two*, Kim couldn't help thinking. But before he could open his mouth to make any further objections, Storm Costello stopped him.

'It's just too noisy at home, Douglas,' she snapped. 'You're in and out all day, banging doors. The phone's always

205

ringing. There's always building work going on somewhere. Then there's the next-door neighbours' damn dog. You know what it's like.'

Kim felt sorry for him. 'Your husband's only trying to help,' she said softly.

'Well in that case he can save me a job by getting that useless wreck of a car towed away and letting me get on with what I do best.'

Perhaps it was the sheer bewilderment on Douglas's face that made Kim come to his rescue. She knew exactly where the car had come off the road from one of the RTA team. Although she hadn't seen it, she knew it had taken a hammering. It would probably take Douglas the whole morning and most of the afternoon to get someone to come and tow it away. It would take her one phone call to Fred at the scrapyard in Dingley and the job would be done.

'Are you sure?' Douglas said when she volunteered to make the call.

'You let me deal with it,' she said. 'Meanwhile, since your wife is obviously determined to stick to her plans, maybe you can drive her over there and settle her in. Perhaps stop at The Crown for a spot of lunch en route. They do a lovely steak.'

Really, she told Michael later, she ought to have chosen the diplomatic service when she was first looking for a job. She was a natural.

* * *

'Have you been round to Dad's yet?'

Why oh why hadn't she checked her phone screen before picking up? Kim was parked outside the station, drinking the dregs of her coffee and waiting. Waiting for what, she didn't know. But when the call came, her response would be rapid.

'Shannon, I'm at work. I've told you before about ringing me here.'

'Well, you can't be that busy or you wouldn't have picked up,' Shannon came back.

She was right, of course. Kim wasn't busy. That was the trouble with this job. You spent half your time driving around, bored silly and longing for someone to commit a crime so you'd get a call to race to the scene; the other half you spent in a total panic because you'd been bombarded with calls demanding your attendance at six different incidents simultaneously.

'So have you been, or what?'

'No. I'm going tonight.' She hadn't planned on it, but anything to get Shannon off her back.

'You make sure you tell him . . . '

'Oh, Shannon. I'm sorry. I think there's something coming over the radio. Looks like it could be an emergency. I'm afraid I'm going to have to cut this convo short.'

She was fibbing. Her radio remained silent. There wasn't even a squawk. But she had had a call on her mobile. It was Toby, who ran the local youth club. Wondering what he wanted, she dialled him back.

They'd only spoken yesterday. Like the public-spirited officer she was, she'd kept her promise and arranged for the removal of Storm Costello's wreck of a car. Only, while she was waiting for the arrival of the haulage truck she'd had a good look at it and decided it wasn't as much of a wreck as she'd been led to believe. That was when she'd had the idea of ringing Toby and persuading him that it was just the kind of car some of his young members might enjoy dismantling and putting back together again.

'Hiya, Toby,' she said. 'How are things? What do the lads think about the car?'

There was a beat. Then, 'I didn't know if I should ring you, Kim. But I've slept on it and well, I thought I should.'

Kim was intrigued. 'What is it?'

'It was while I was stripping it,' he said. 'The car, I mean.'

'What about it?'

'That accident you told me about. It looks to me like it wasn't an accident after all. I'd say someone had been tampering with the driver's brake linings.'

*   *   *

As soon as Kim put the duty sarge in the picture about Toby's phone call, he ordered her to come back to the station right away. If the damage to Storm Costello's brakes had been deliberate, then they might very well be looking at a case of attempted murder. And if the intended victim — just out of hospital and vulnerable — was staying alone in her rented cottage in the middle of nowhere, then someone was going to need to pay her a visit to check on her. That someone, so the sarge informed her, might as well be Kim. But before she set off for Owl Cottage, the super apparently wanted a word.

It was with some trepidation that Kim knocked on the super's door. She didn't know why she always felt so nervous whenever she found herself in Chris Cleaver's presence. She was a perfectly pleasant woman, unlike some high-rankers she'd found herself working under, who enjoyed nothing more than throwing their weight around when in the presence of mere PCs.

Kim wondered if her nervousness might be something to do with the super's high expectations of everyone who stood before her. She hated sloppiness — be it in manner, dress or speech — and though she could never be accused of being an unsympathetic boss, whatever personal problems you might be suffering, it was taken for granted you left them at home.

When Kim entered the room, she was in the middle of watering a rather desperate-looking houseplant, her face set in a mask of deep concentration. Once she'd finished her task, she set down the plastic bottle she'd been using as a watering can and turned to speak.

'So, since — so I've been informed — you're the only one round here to have met this Storm Costello, what impression did you come away with?' she said, quickly moving onto the nitty-gritty once the pleasantries were out of the way. 'For instance, did you get the idea she was frightened of her husband?'

The question caught Kim unawares, although she ought to have guessed that Chris would be several steps ahead of her. And, thankfully, it was an easy one to answer.

'I'd have said not,' she replied without a moment's hesitation. 'She seemed a bit dismissive of him, if anything. Sending him off to find a nurse to sort the flowers out I'd brought, that sort of thing.'

'You brought her flowers? Surely that was above and beyond the call of duty PC Stone?'

She didn't think she'd imagined the smile in Chris's voice. As briefly as she could, she explained her connection with Storm Costello through Michael and that the flowers had been a get-well present from him. And just in case she found herself being questioned further about why *she'd* taken them and not him, she made certain to emphasise the fact that she was there for less than ten minutes and that the hospital was en route to her intended destination half a mile away.

'She writes crime novels, doesn't she?' the super said, turning back to her plant and fastidiously picking off a papery yellow leaf. The dead leaf was one of many, actually. Kim couldn't resist the thought that it was a good job Chris Cleaver was a high-flying police officer and not a horticulturalist.

'That's right, ma'am.'

'Read any, have you?'

Kim shook her head.

'Me neither. Can't get on with them,' the super replied. 'Something to do with the detectives in them. They all seem to lead such complicated lives outside the job. Totally unrealistic, if you ask me.'

Kim smiled.

'As if we have either the time or the energy to do anything once we've got home in this job,' she added.

Snap went another dead leaf.

'So she wasn't frightened of him, yet she didn't want to go home with him,' the super went on. 'Do you think she was telling the truth when she said she just needed space to write?'

Kim couldn't work out if the super were actually asking her opinion or simply thinking aloud. In response, she attempted an articulation in her throat that could have been interpreted as one of either agreement or consideration. Or possibly both. Though she suspected it sounded more like she was being strangled.

'We're going to have to interview him of course,' Chris said.

She marched over to her desk and sat

down in front of her computer.

'Though since there are no spare bodies around right now, it'll have to wait,' she said. 'It's hardly at the top of my list of priorities at the moment,' she added with a sigh.

'Fingers crossed he doesn't try anything else then before one of the DCs becomes available,' Kim said.

The super looked up from her screen and frowned at Kim's words. 'You know, I'm wondering if I should be sending you round to Storm Costello's place alone, Kim.'

It had crossed Kim's mind too. Undaunted, she stood tall and fixed the super with a steady gaze. 'What choice do we have?'

The super gave a shrug of defeat. Kim was right, of course.

'Just don't put yourself in any danger. No heroics, okay?'

That was the protocol. But what if curiosity got the better of her? Could she honestly promise to wait outside and do nothing till backup arrived, while who knew what might be going on inside? Or worse still, knowing that something might already have happened?

*   *   *

When Kim arrived at Owl Cottage, she didn't know whether to be relieved or nervous to see no sign of Burgess's car. Once out of the driver's seat, she closed the door soundlessly behind her and thought about what to do next. She tried not to think about Douglas Burgess possibly paying his wife a second call and this time doing a better job of getting rid of her.

She was being dramatic, was all. This was Lenton Wood, she reminded herself. The heart of the English countryside. It had won awards for being litter-free. A minor royal had presented a trophy to the leader of the church council, and the local newspaper had done a piece about how villages like this one encapsulated community values. It had even been on the local TV news.

Straightening her cap, Kim took her courage in her hands and strolled up to

215

the front door. She stood there for a few seconds, straining her ears for any sound coming from inside. Was it good or bad that there was none?

She rapped hard on the brass owl-shaped knocker. As she waited for a response, she looked around her. Owl Cottage was certainly the perfect location for carrying out dark deeds. It was set back from the road, hidden from the nearest house by high walls and shady trees. The front garden was mostly tarmacked, but what about the back? How far did it stretch? she wondered. Did it contain a deep well? Or maybe it was laid to earth with a lean-to shed nearby that contained a convenient spade for a spot of grave digging? There she was, letting her imagination run riot again.

She was thinking about trying the side gate when she heard footsteps and the sound of bolts being drawn back, followed by several locks being turned. All this seemed to go on forever before the door finally opened to reveal Storm Costello. Today she was swathed in a purple kaftan that stopped short of two rather puffy ankles. Into a pair of silver open-toed sandals were squeezed two broad feet, each toenail painted blood-red. She looked anxious, Kim thought.

'May I come inside, Ms Costello?'

Storm Costello stood aside to let her in and she followed her down the low-ceilinged narrow hallway into another equally low-ceilinged room. Whoever owned this place was clearly determined to plug the countryside angle as strongly as possible. The walls were studded with pictures of typical country scenes — the local hunt in pursuit of a desperate fox; a flock of grazing sheep, a pair of lovers wandering through woodland hand in hand. It was all very chocolate-box, Kim thought.

'Thankfully the rest of the house is a lot less distracting,' Storm Costello said, following Kim's gaze. 'Otherwise I wouldn't get a single word written.'

Ah yes, the novel. Kim asked her how it was coming along.

'Oh, you know.' Storm waved Kim's question away dismissively. 'You don't want to hear about that. Actually, I was just getting down to it when you arrived, so if you could be brief . . . '

'Of course.'

Kim decided she might as well come straight out with it. Storm Costello wasn't averse to a bit of plain speaking herself, so why should she be? 'We believe someone deliberately tampered with your brakes,' she said. 'And it was this that caused your accident the other evening.'

Ms Costello sat down heavily on the nearest settee, a chintzy affair covered in blooms. She was clearly a woman not easily frightened, and she was no idiot. From her expression, it struck Kim she'd already made the leap between what she'd just been told and the implication of the words. Which kind of made her job a little easier.

'I hate to have to ask, but do you have any reason to believe someone might be out to harm you?' she said.

'No,' Storm said. 'Of course not.'

'Well then, has anything happened recently, however small and insignificant seeming at the time, that's made you feel you might be in danger?'

There was a moment's hesitation before Storm spoke again, during which time she removed her glasses and breathed on the lenses before she began vigorously polishing them on the sleeve of her kaftan.

'I'm not leaving this place,' Storm said. 'I've paid the lease for six weeks.'

It was a strange reply. Personally, if Kim had suspected someone might be out to get her, she'd gladly lose her deposit. But then, what if she felt she had nowhere to go but home, and it was home where the greatest danger lay?

'You haven't answered my question,' she said.

'Because it's a ridiculous one,' Storm replied.

'You could go back home.' She studied Storm Costello for any change in her demeanour as she spoke the words. And she was pretty sure she'd seen her flinch.

'Absolutely not!'

There followed more vigorous polishing. What was she avoiding? Kim wondered. 'Ms Costello, are you afraid of your husband?'

Storm widened her eyes. 'Afraid of Dougie? Seriously?' She threw her head back and gave a tinkling laugh. 'You've met my husband, haven't you, Officer?' she said.

'Briefly.'

'Then you'll know he's a pussycat. For a start, in order to murder me he'd have to pay me a visit, and he's been told what will happen to him if he does.'

Kim said nothing to this. She simply counted in her head the number of women who'd told her a similar story of trust and devotion where it hadn't ended well for them.

'And there's no need to look at me like that,' Storm said. 'I'm not one of your domestic violence victims.'

As soon as Storm rose from the settee, Kim knew the conversation was over. There was nothing she could do against such stubbornness. But before she found herself corralled in the direction of the front door, she handed over a panic alarm. Maybe the sight of one of these could drive home the fact that she might be in some danger.

'If at any time you feel yourself to be in danger, press this,' she said. 'You won't even need to speak. Officers will be round in no time.'

Storm took it with her manicured hand, glanced at it with some disdain, then dropped it on the hall table dismissively. Then, with a curt goodbye, Kim found herself on the other side of the door.

*   *   *

Back in the car, she lay her forearms on the wheel and rested her head on them. Storm Costello had wiped the floor with her. But what else could she have done? There was no evidence to suggest Douglas Burgess had committed any crime against his wife. And yet she'd refused point blank to return to the marital home.

It was all very disturbing. The super had been right. They should have sent a detective. All this stuff was way outside Kim's job description. And the one thing that kept running through her mind was, if anything *did* happen to Storm Costello at her husband's hands, who would be taking the rap for it? From where she was sitting, it looked very much like it might be herself.

It was a relief when her phone rang. Dad's name flashed up on the screen and all thoughts of Storm Costello vanished from her mind. This was an emergency. Dad *never* rang. *She* rang Dad. Before Mum had died she'd ring Mum, who'd then relay her message back to Dad. If he had a reply other than a grunt, then it would come back via Mum.

'Dad, what is it? Are you okay?' Already she was imagining every kind of accident. At the very least, he'd had a minor stroke.

'I am and I'm not,' he said.

What did that mean?

'I've had your sister on to me.'

Shannon. Of course. She already knew what was coming next. She'd ignored her sister's plea to go round to Dad's and dissuade him from going any further with his new lady friend. So Shannon had gone round there herself.

'Your sister seems to think I'm in the

clutches of a fortune hunter,' he said.

At least he sounded as if he could see the funny side. Kim swapped panicking for seething. What she wanted to do most right now was to get on the phone to Shannon and tear her off several strips.

But the two of them had made a pact — albeit one Shannon often forgot when it was convenient — that under no circumstances were they ever to slag each other off to their parents. Right now Kim was fighting the urge not to go back on the pact herself. A few deep breaths and she'd pushed the thought right out of her mind.

'She's only being protective, Dad,' Kim said.

'Is that another word for meddlesome? Ellen's a friend, that's all.'

Ellen. So the fortune hunter had a name.

'If she's not careful, she'll end up pushing us into each other's arms,' Dad said. 'It'll be like Romeo and Juliet all over again.'

Kim couldn't resist a smile. 'Do you want me to have a word?'

'No. I've a better idea. Come round for tea today. Then you can meet Ellen for yourself.'

'Well, I for one would love to. What about Shannon? Has she agreed?'

'I've not asked her. That can be your job.'

It was a relief to discover that Dad's telephone habits hadn't changed that much. One phone call was obviously enough for one day. Probably for one week. She was just about to say so when a dark figure loomed up at the window, blocking her view. It was a man, and his large hairy-knuckled fist was about to make contact with her window. Immediately Kim was on her guard. Whoever it was, she was ready for him.

'Dad, I've got to go,' she said, cutting him off mid-complaint. 'I'll text you later.'

She flung open the car door, too slow to catch her would-be assailant, who'd managed to hop out of reach of the metal.

'You!'

'Well, there's nothing wrong with your reactions.'

DC Noel Harper, looking even more rakish than ever, stood on one leg, rubbing his other ankle fiercely. He needed a shave and there were bags under his eyes you could carry a week's shopping in; and as for his jacket, well the least said about that the better.

'The super sent me,' he said. 'Apparently she's got you on her conscience. Everything okay here?'

'It was fine till you came along and scared me half witless,' she said.

'Yeah, sorry about that.'

'You're forgiven.' Kim said with a smile. 'So where now?'

'You and me are going to pay a visit to Douglas Burgess's place,' he said. 'I think he needs to answer a few questions. And on the way there, you can fill me in on this writer woman.'

★ ★ ★

Just how good an actor *was* Douglas Burgess? At first, when Noel informed him that his wife's brake cables had been tampered with, he looked puzzled, like someone failing to comprehend the significance. A moment in, however, and the penny finally dropped.

'You think someone deliberately wanted her to have an accident?' he said.

'We don't know, Mr Burgess,' Kim said. 'That's why we're here. We thought you might be able to help us with that.'

'How?' His gaze switched from Noel to Kim and back to Noel again. Finally he seemed to realise. 'You don't think I did it, I hope!'

'No one is accusing anyone of anything,' Noel said in his most reassuring tone.

'Good,' Burgess said. 'At least we've got that straight.' He gestured for them to sit down but remained standing himself. He was a pacer, this one, Kim saw. Up and down the carpet he went, thinking his thoughts, whatever they were. It was obvious his nerves were all over the place. He wasn't doing himself any favours.

'These brake linings. How do you know about them? And where are they now?'

His question was directed at Noel, who

226

replied as politely and concisely as he could that a) he wasn't at liberty to say how they knew about the brake linings and b) that the evidence was safely locked away.

While Noel delivered his reply, Kim had the opportunity to get the measure of the living room into which Douglas Burgess had led them, his big bearded face initially welcoming as he'd opened the front door to admit them.

It was a mess, that was for sure. It looked like Burgess had eaten all his meals in here since his wife's departure and hadn't bothered clearing any of the remains away. She couldn't imagine what Storm Costello's reaction would be were she to walk in right now. Or rather, she could imagine it all too easily.

'Does my wife know about this?' asked Burgess.

Kim assured him that she'd been to see her personally.

'What? You mean you knocked on her door, told her somebody might be trying to kill her, then got back in your car and drove away?'

227

He did good outrage, there was no denying it. She wondered about mentioning the alarm she'd let Storm have. How would possessing that information make him feel, though? Hesitant about making a return trip in case Storm decided to summon immediate help and he was caught red-handed? Or confident by being forewarned? Before she could decide, Noel spoke.

'My colleague here asked Ms Costello if she knew of anyone who might want to do her any harm,' he said.

'Well I hoped she gave you that woman's name.'

Kim and Noel exchanged wary glances.

'She didn't, did she?' Burgess said, glaring at the two of them. 'I might have known it. Weeks it's been going on and all I get from Storm is, 'Don't worry, she's just a lonely star-struck fan.' And now this.'

'Are you saying that someone's been bothering your wife, sir?' Noel said.

'Bothering her? Bothering her?' A fleck of spittle flew from Burgess's lips. 'Someone's been stalking my wife for months now,' he said. 'And I can give you her name.'

★   ★   ★

There was something spectral about Diana Corbett, Kim thought. When she spoke, every muscle in her face was visible. The veins sat too near the surface of her arms, and with each movement she made, the outline of the bones revealed themselves.

She hadn't been living in the flat long, she said, once all three of them were seated in her lounge. So she hoped they'd forgive the jumble of boxes stacked around the living room. The boxes were the first thing Kim had noticed. Box upon box of books. Another bookworm, she'd thought. Just like Michael.

There was little else here that gave away what kind of person Diana Corbett might be. The furniture was nondescript — cheap and cheerful and chosen by a landlord obviously more influenced by cost than design. And as for the bare walls, they either revealed that she had no interest in art and no family photos to display, or they could just mean that her pictures and photos were something else she'd not yet got round to unpacking.

There'd been a mix-up at the door about why they were here to see her. Had they come about the neighbour from her last place? she'd wanted to know. When it became apparent that they hadn't a clue what she was talking about, she said it didn't matter. It was ancient history now anyway, since as they could see, she'd moved away from the old place.

She'd heard about the accident, she said, when Noel said they were actually here to ask her a few questions about Storm Costello. In fact, she'd been at the library the other evening expecting to hear Storm's talk, and she recognised Kim as the police officer who'd come inside and told them what had happened.

Kim, who for her part had no memory at all of Diana, said something innocuous about the size of the audience and the difficulty of picking out individual faces, which seemed to satisfy Miss Corbett. Except she was still puzzled about why they were asking her about Storm Costello, she said, leading them into her living room and offering them each a seat.

'We can't comment about that,' Noel said, once seated. 'For now I'd just like to know how well you know her.'

In her small face, Diana Corbett's eyes looked huge. 'Not at all, really,' she said. 'I joined her writing class when I first moved back here from London.'

It had been her lifeline, she said. She'd moved to be nearer family but had ended up regretting it, as it turned out she had nothing in common with any of them.

'I'd just decided I'd made the biggest mistake of my life moving back to Orton when I saw the notice about the writers' group,' she said, her wan face relaxing into a contented smile. 'It changed everything.'

'Tell me about it,' Kim said. 'How many of you are there?'

'About twelve, though not everyone attends regularly. I never miss it though, even when I'm at my worst.'

She had a heart condition, she explained, when Kim gave her a curious look. It meant she was often too tired to do much. But the thought of the evening class always reinvigorated her. Storm sounded like an excellent teacher, Noel said. She was, Diana agreed. She'd even kept Diana back on occasions, to discuss her writing. 'My paltry efforts' was how she'd described it self-deprecatingly.

So Diana spent more time with Storm than your average attendee. But did that mark her out as a stalker?

'How often does the group meet?' Kim asked.

'Once a week on a Monday,' Diana said. 'Between seven and nine at Storm's house.' It had to be Mondays, she added, because that was the night Storm's husband went out to his evening class. 'Motor vehicle maintenance at the FE college or something equally manly,' she said, quite disdainfully Kim thought. 'Sometimes I'm still there when he gets in. I'm sure he thinks I'm stalking her.'

Kim and Noel exchanged a glance. It hadn't escaped Diana's keen eye.

'Has there been a complaint about me?' she asked, her voice suddenly rising in pitch. 'Is that why you're here?'

Neither of them spoke.

'Sometimes it's difficult for me to know where the boundaries are,' she said. 'Perhaps I stay a bit too long when it's time to go and everyone else has already left.' On the few occasions Douglas Burgess had come home and found Diana and Storm deep in conversation, he'd made no effort to hide his disapproval, she admitted. 'But if Storm had wanted me to go, then she would have told me.' She raised her eyes from her thin hands, which she'd been twisting and twisting in her lap as she stared pleadingly at Kim. 'She would, wouldn't she?'

When Kim failed to reply, Diana let out a sound of despair. 'Oh, God,' she said. 'She wouldn't, would she? She's far too kind. I expect she just puts up with me, just like . . . '

She stopped there. Just like who? Kim wondered. It occurred to her that Diana Corbett was lonely. She'd already admitted she didn't get on with her family, and presumably she had few friends, since she'd only just moved from London. Perhaps it had been her loneliness that had made her latch onto Storm Costello the way she had. It would have been easy for Burgess to make her out to be some crazy old stalker spinster in order to fit her up as a possible suspect for fiddling with his wife's brakes.

But what possible motive could she have had for killing Storm, who'd gone out of her way to encourage her? Burgess, on the other hand, attended a weekly course in motor mechanics. Presumably the course covered something about brake linings.

★ ★ ★

'So what did you think of the new flame?'

Kim had given Shannon a lift home. En route, they'd stopped at the chippy and treated themselves. Now they sat in Kim's car, chomping their way through haddock and chips. The only sound was some quiet munching and the rustle of paper as each dug into their food. It was bliss. Unfortunately, Shannon was a quick eater. The silence didn't last long.

Kim had been waiting for this. The post-mortem. Tea with Dad and his new girlfriend had been a tense overly polite affair for the most part. Dad had made a cake, but it had sunk, which had put him into a sulk. Ellen had made a great show of saying how delicious it was and had eaten two pieces to prove it.

Kim had thought her quite sweet, actually. And she liked the way she'd told Dad off for making such a fuss. It was just a cake, she said. So what if it wasn't up to his usual standard? There'd be other, better ones. Of course this hadn't gone down at all well with Shannon, who didn't say anything, but it was clear she thought the new woman was being overly familiar.

She hadn't liked it, either, that Ellen was more interested in Kim's job in the police force than she was in Shannon and her girls. Like Diana Corbett, Ellen Murphy had also been at the event on Monday night. If she'd realised who Kim was, she would have come over and introduced herself, she said.

Kim couldn't believe her luck when she discovered that Ellen had also been a member of Storm's writing group. What a fantastic opportunity to do a bit of digging about the rather odd Diana Corbett, she thought. Alas, Ellen had only gone along there for the first three weeks. It soon became apparent, once she'd seen what the other members of the group could pull off, that she couldn't write for toffee. So she'd left and taken up yoga instead.

Of course Shannon's nose was put thoroughly out of joint with all this, and it wasn't long before she began making noises about going home. Since Kim was the one with the transport, she'd had no other choice but to comply with her sister's wishes.

Her mind kept drifting back to that earlier visit to Diana's and what she'd said when they'd first arrived. She'd wanted to know if they'd come about the neighbour. And then later she'd admitted it wasn't the first time she'd been accused of getting too familiar with someone. Perhaps if she went back to the station right now, she could have a dig around and see if she could locate the complaint Diana Corbett's erstwhile neighbour had made against her.

'You haven't been listening to a word I've said, have you?' Shannon was making a big thing of screwing up her fish and chip wrappings. 'I said Her Ladyship has a long way to go before she can possibly match our mother.'

Kim rolled her eyes as she chased the last chip with her wooden fork. 'Are you still talking about this?' she sighed.

'I'm upset,' Shannon said.

'Well don't be. Let Dad make his own mistakes. And stop being so sarky about her.'

'What do you mean, sarky?'

'Her name's Ellen. Not Her Ladyship or Lady Muck or Madam or any of the other the names you've come out with since you found out about her.' Kim popped the last chip in her mouth and ate it with slow relish.

'I was only saying,' Shannon mumbled.

'Listen, I'm afraid I've got to let you out now, Shannon,' she said, leaning over to open the door on her sister's side. 'I've just remembered there's something I forgot to do at work.' She flashed Shannon a warm smile but failed to get one back. Now she was in a mood that could last a week till Kim apologised. Honestly, her sister could take umbrage for England. 'Ring me in the week,' she said sweetly.

But Shannon had gone, banging the door loudly and leaving behind her leftovers for Kim to dispose of. It was her idea of the last word, Kim thought philosophically as she drove off in the direction of the police station.

It was quiet at the station. Had it been a Friday night, of course, they'd be bringing the first of the drunks in. But Wednesdays were quiet locally. It might well be two in the morning by the time anything of note happened. By that time, Kim would be well and truly tucked up in her bed. Her next night shift was days away, thank goodness.

She had a brief exchange with the duty sergeant before going on the hunt for a spare computer. People had funny ideas about what it was like to be a serving police officer, she mused, when after a hunt that lasted a good ten minutes she finally located one and began her search for Diana Corbett. The popular image of a British bobby was of a man or woman chasing criminals on the streets of England. The reality was a bank of computers and a copper seated at every one. How times had changed.

It didn't take long to find what she was looking for. According to the case file, Diana had caught her neighbour, a Miss Hilda Rudge, wandering up and down the street one day, having locked herself out. The old lady had been cold and quite distressed, so Diana had taken her into her own house and arranged for a locksmith to get access to the house and change the locks. When she suggested she should hold a spare key for safekeeping, Miss Rudge, a woman in her late seventies, had agreed, according to Diana.

Miss Rudge had also agreed to let Diana have her old bike, which she kept in the shed. Gave it her for free, in fact, so

Diana said, since the old lady hadn't been able to ride it herself for years. It had needed some repairs, for which Diana had ended up paying, but it was still cheaper than buying a brand-new bike; and anyway, Miss Snape had been insistent, her statement continued.

'I thought we were friends,' she'd written. 'It came as a shock when Miss Rudge reported me to the police for failing to return her bike after she said she'd only loaned it to me and for breaking into her house, which was nonsense.'

She'd readily admitted she'd let herself in on a couple of occasions — both times because she couldn't get an answer when she knocked and the milk was still outside on the step, she said. But she hoped the police would agree that she was only being neighbourly. If social services had been a bit prompter and come out to assess the old lady on the occasion she'd called them instead of promising to come and failing, she said, then she'd never have interfered. The police, it seemed, had agreed with her. Miss Snape, apparently, was now in the care of the local authority and the case was closed.

So that was that. Diana was off the hook. Kim felt sorry for her. No wonder she'd decided to move. And no wonder she was on her guard in the presence of the police, in case any overtures she made towards anyone else might be misconstrued as stalking.

Having got to the bottom of this story made her wonder if perhaps it was time to go back and pay Douglas another visit. Especially with this added information about how he spent his Monday evenings.

It was thinking about him that made her take the turning into the long wide street where he lived with Storm Costello when she wasn't hiding out in the middle of the countryside. She drove slowly, hoping to see what, she didn't know. Perhaps Douglas throwing a rope and spade into the boot of his car before he drove off towards Owl Cottage.

In the event, she saw nothing. The house was in darkness, and Douglas's car, which she'd last spotted parked in the driveway, wasn't there. Kim yawned. It had been a long day. What she wanted more than ever was to get out of this uniform and into a long hot bath.

★ ★ ★

'I suppose you heard about last night?'

The next morning, Kim was getting her flat white coffee from the machine in readiness for the day ahead. Except the machine had decided to offer her a cappuccino with extra sprinkles instead. She tore her mind away from the email of complaint to the manufacturers of this machine she was mentally composing, to see Noel standing there.

'Tell me,' she said, scowling at her coffee.

'Storm Costello,' he said. 'First response team got the panic button.'

'No! What happened? Is she all right?'

'As far as I know.' He'd just been getting the lowdown from one of the crew who went out there, he told her. 'She'd panicked because she'd imagined an intruder trying to get into her house at the back,' he said.

'What do you mean by 'imagined'? Was there an intruder or wasn't there one?'

Noel shrugged. They'd had a good look round, apparently. Even ventured into the woods backing onto the house. But they'd found no trace of anyone.

'So what happens now?' Kim said. 'Surely she can't be allowed to stay there on her own. Would she even want to?'

'I think they persuaded her to call a friend in the end,' Noel said. 'She said something about ringing her agent, who was also a good friend.'

That was a relief, at least. Another thought suddenly occurred to Kim. 'What time was this, by the way? When it all kicked off, I mean.'

'Round half nine when they got the call, I think.'

'Well, that's funny,' she said, 'because I happened to be driving past Douglas Burgess's place around that time, and not only was the house in total darkness, but his car wasn't there either.'

Noel fixed her with a look that suggested he was more than mildly interested. What had she been doing down there? he wanted to know. Briefly she filled him in on her off-duty sojourn researching Diana Corbett and the conclusion she'd reached.

'I'd say it lets Diana off the hook as far as stalking Storm Costello goes, wouldn't you?'

'Pretty much,' he said. 'Being a bit odd isn't against the law. Not yet, anyway.'

'So what do we do now?' Kim asked.

'Onward and upward,' he said. 'Personally I'd like to hear a bit more about what Burgess does in in his motor vehicle maintenance class.'

★ ★ ★

The police had left now, and Storm was all alone. She sat at her desk in the small back room she'd appropriated as a study. It was the one with the least fussy curtains and the fewest pictures. Any pictures there had been, she'd taken down and stashed under the bed. All those busy landscapes were just too distracting.

This room looked out over the wood

behind the house. It was dark. Really dark, unlike her own suburban street where there was always the light of someone's house or a street lamp to see by. With the dark and the wind, no wonder she'd been spooked. Spooked enough to press that button that had brought the police rushing over in no time. They hadn't found anyone, of course, but she'd known they wouldn't.

She'd promised to ring Tina. Told them she'd done so, in fact. You might feel more at ease if you ring a friend to come and stay with you, the nice policeman had said. She'd ring Tina Cash, her agent, she'd replied. In fact, she'd do it now, she'd promised, while he was drinking his tea and warming himself by her fire.

He'd offered to wait until Tina came, but Storm insisted it wouldn't be necessary. Her friend had already left her house and would be with her in no time, she said. If he was reluctant to leave, it was only because the house was so warm and not because he put her safety before all else, she was sure of that. As far as he was concerned, she was just one more batty woman with an overactive imagination.

Telling him that Tina was en route was another lie, of course. She hadn't even rung her. Tina was the last person she'd call if ever she was in need of help. She could just imagine the conversation.

'Darling. Lovely to hear from you. Now, how's the novel coming along?'

'Oh, just fine. Only a few finishing touches left.'

Storm opened her laptop. An eerie green light flickered across the screen as she logged on, casting ghostly shadows round the room. At home she'd usually spend a good fifteen minutes playing around on the internet before she opened any document. But the Wi-Fi at Owl Cottage was chancy, and tonight it had decided to pack in entirely.

So now she had no excuse but to get to work. The reason she'd given everyone — Dougie, her writing class, Tina of course — for cancelling all her commitments until it was all but complete. She'd done a marvellous job of convincing them she was well on the way with it, even down to her refusal to reveal the title. She didn't want to jinx it, she'd told them all.

This was the biggest lie of all. Click, went the mouse, on the document she'd entitled simply NOVEL. There was no novel. Only the simple heading Chapter One, followed by blank page after blank page.

★ ★ ★

If ever a man was determined to make two police officers unwelcome, then that man was Douglas Burgess. He cracked the door open just wide enough to reveal half his face. One suspicious eye, one unsmiling mouth.

'It's not all that convenient just now,' he said when Noel asked if they could come inside.

Noel was an affable chap as a rule. But Douglas had caught him on a bad day. 'We could do this at the station if you prefer,' he snapped.

They gave him just enough time for Noel's words to sink in. When they had, he stepped aside to let them in. 'What's it about this time?' he said.

Kim looked past him into the kitchen. It looked like he'd been on a bit of a cleaning spree. Same in the lounge too, she thought as he ushered them in there. Before getting out of the car, Kim and Noel had agreed that he should be the one to do the talking. Today she was the eyes. This was what had put Noel in a bad mood, actually. He'd left his glasses at home, and he hated having to admit that without them he was rubbish.

'Have you had any more contact with your wife since we last saw you?' Noel asked.

Douglas frowned. He hadn't, he said. On his wife's orders. He'd not even texted or phoned her. She got so cross when she was interrupted, he said, that he'd long since learned to ignore the DO NOT DISTURB sign she hung on her door at his peril.

'Your wife called the police last night,' Noel went on. 'She said she thought she'd seen someone hanging round the back of the property she's currently renting.'

'Well it wasn't me,' Douglas said.

Not, Kim noticed, 'Oh, dear, how is she, is she safe?'

'Where were you yesterday evening, Mr Burgess?' Noel asked.

'Me? I was here of course.'

'All evening?'

'From about six, yes. That's when I got in from work. I'd set aside last night to do a bit of cleaning. I've let things slide a bit since Storm left me on my own.'

'And what time did you go to bed?'

Douglas gazed into the middle distance. He couldn't say for sure, he said, but since he usually went to bed immediately the closing theme tune to *Newsnight* began, then he could only surmise that it would have been round eleven fifteen.

'That van of yours parked outside in the drive,' Noel said, 'do you put it in the garage at night?'

The look on Douglas's face matched that of someone who'd immediately twigged that there was a right answer and a wrong one. Sadly, he'd not yet worked out which was which, and the detective wasn't giving any hints.

'Not as a rule,' he said. 'It's safe enough out there.'

'And last night?'

He shrugged. He couldn't remember, he said. Nice one, Kim mused. Hedging might work. For a short while, at least.

'But if — as a rule — you don't lock it up, then it's pretty safe to assume that last night was no exception?'

Douglas didn't reply. In fact, he appeared to have given up speaking. In Kim's experience of confronting people with something to hide, you could divide them into two groups: those who were suddenly struck dumb, and those who became so garrulous you couldn't shut them up. Right now, she didn't know if Douglas Burgess was guilty of trying to kill his wife by messing with her brakes, nor could she swear that he was guilty of prowling around Owl Cottage in the dark. But she was sure of this — he was definitely guilty of something. With a bit of luck, they'd soon find out what it was.

'When my colleague here drove past your house last night around half past nine,' Noel said, 'it was in darkness and there was no sign of your car.'

Douglas opened his mouth to speak but immediately closed it again.

'So where were you?'

Douglas put his two hands together as if in prayer and brought them to his lips.

'OK. I wasn't here,' he said from behind his hands. 'But I wasn't at Owl Cottage either.'

Kim would never have maintained that she was blessed with second sight. But what Douglas said next didn't surprise her for one minute.

'I was with somebody,' he said. 'Another woman.'

It was as if Douglas's confession had broken the seal on his lips. Out they came, a tumble of words tripping over each other, occasionally snagging on a repetitive groove before tugging themselves free and flying off in another direction altogether. He knew what it looked like, he said. But he hadn't invited it. If 'the other woman' had come into his life at any other time, then he wouldn't even have given her the time of day. He'd been patient with Storm for as long as he was able to be. He'd put up with her strops, kept out of her way so she could have the peace and quiet she demanded in order to write, cooked her meals, never complained. But all he got in return were temper tantrums and accusations that he didn't understand her artistic nature.

'We were happy once,' he said. 'Though I know from the outside it must have looked like we had nothing in common. Okay, yeah, we were from different worlds. But we fitted together like a hand in a glove.'

He was an odd job man by trade, he said. Left school at sixteen, and unlike Storm, he'd barely read a book. Storm had picked up his card from her doormat one day and called him. She might be able to write novels, he explained, but she was totally impractical. Apparently she was always asking him if something would work in one of her plots as a way to kill someone. There was nothing wrong with her imagination, he'd give her that much, he said, even if she sometimes got the practicalities wrong. Perhaps realising that his words might be seen as incriminating, he quickly changed the subject.

'The first thing I fixed was her dripping kitchen tap,' he said. 'The week after, something else went wrong, and she called me up to fix that too.' There was always something, he said. And generally he was able to fix it. When the job was complete, she'd make him a cup of tea and they'd chat. 'We sort of clicked. She was good company. Good-natured. Fun to be with. At least for the first couple of years.' But recently things had changed between them, he went on. 'She's been under a lot of pressure,' he said. 'This last book hasn't been easy, and I know the reviews stung.'

Given the ones she'd read herself, Kim could well understand that.

'She's lost a lot of confidence,' he said. 'Hates everything she writes. She's terrified her agent will drop her when she sees the new novel.'

But none of this was his fault, he said. When she took her frustration out on him, he simply put up with it. All he wanted was for her to stop being so miserable and start enjoying life again.

'It was my idea to get her to start the writing group,' he said. 'I thought it might remind her why she'd started writing in the first place. Because she loved words and had always had so many stories to tell.'

Except, he added, the writing group only added to her misery. It swallowed her time. She got so involved in other people's writing she no longer had any time for her own.

'That was why she decided to rent Owl Cottage, so she could immerse herself in her new book,' he said.

Kim wondered when he was going to bring up the subject of the other woman. She hadn't long to wait. To Kim's ears it sounded like a rerun of the first time he'd met Storm. Except this time, it wasn't a dripping tap but a dodgy cupboard door that wouldn't stay shut.

'Tell me, Mr Burgess,' Kim couldn't resist asking him, 'you say you're a handyman. Does that include an ability to take a car apart and put it back together again?'

'Look, I did not interfere with the

brake cables on my wife's car,' he said. 'I wouldn't even know where to find the damn things, for a start. I'll admit to being a practical man, but I've always preferred to leave cars to the expert.'

'Except you've been enrolled in a car maintenance class for the last six weeks,' Noel said. 'We've checked.'

Kim's gaze flickered over the bookshelves Douglas was standing in front of. Books, books, books. Everyone she'd met recently was up to their ears in them. She screwed up her eyes to read the titles, waiting for Douglas's response.

'Well, you've done your homework, I'll give you that,' he said after a long pause. 'Except, have you actually checked the register?'

Kim swung her gaze away from the bookshelf. No, they hadn't.

'Thought not,' Douglas said. If they had, he added, then they'd have discovered he'd never actually attended. 'I joined because I needed an excuse,' he said. 'Monday night was my night with her.'

'The same woman you were with last

night?' Kim asked.

He nodded. They'd been to the cinema to see *La-La Land*, he said, then gone for a curry and back to her place. He hadn't come home till this morning.

'You'll have receipts?' Noel asked. 'Cinema tickets? Restaurant bill?'

'Of course,' said Douglas.

'And it goes without saying we'll need the name and address of the lady in question,' Kim said. 'In order to check your alibi.'

Douglas nodded. 'She lives at 14, Hale End Avenue, Orton,' he said.

'And her name?' said Kim.

'Ellen Murphy.'

⋆ ⋆ ⋆

Kim could barely remember how she'd got back outside and into the car. She did remember telling Noel that if it was all the same with him, she'd prefer not to be the one to pay Ellen Murphy a visit. Someone else could go and check out her alibi. Thankfully, Noel hadn't pushed it, but simply drove her back to the station, where she jumped into the nearest patrol car alongside Sally Hardman, who was looking for a partner to go out with.

What with one thing and another — breaking up a fight between a gang of lads outside Chickin Lickin' and coming to the assistance of Mr Khan at the Midan Asian Foods grocery store, who'd locked a shoplifter in his back room — a young woman who, in the twenty minutes she was in there, had succeeded in consuming all the evidence, apart from the tinned stuff — Kim had had no further time to contemplate Douglas Burgess's revelation about Ellen Murphy. She enjoyed working with Sally, who was still new enough in the job to be super-enthusiastic about it. It turned out she'd been one half of the team charged with dealing with Hilda Rudge's complaint against Diana Corbett. The other half had been Shaun Brennan, an old-timer who'd been in the force fifteen years. It was clear Sally resented Shaun.

'After we'd been out there a couple of times and got thoroughly confused at the two women's differing testimonies, Shaun didn't want to get involved any further.'

Apparently he was convinced that Hilda Rudge was suffering from Alzheimer's even if it hadn't yet been diagnosed, and he thought the best people to deal with the case was social services, she said.

'Shaun's an experienced officer,' Kim reminded her. 'He was probably right.'

'Trouble is though,' Sally said, 'he *knows* he's right. Do you know how annoying that can be?'

Kim gave a chuckle.

'Anyway, that Diana Corbett is weird if you ask me,' Sally said. 'She creaks when she walks and she gets right up in your face when she talks. Gave me the creeps, if I'm honest.'

Just then, a call came through asking for any patrol car in the vicinity of 24, Oxford Road to attend an urgent incident. One of these days, Kim thought as they put on the blue light, Sally would learn, just as she had, that sometimes the worst kind of criminal was the one with the big blue eyes and the baby face.

Her shift was over, and now she and Michael were sitting in front of the TV watching a documentary about China. Or rather, Michael was watching it. Kim could only stare at the screen. Occasionally she'd make the odd grunt of acknowledgement in reply to a passing comment of Michael's. It went on like this until the second ad break came along, when Michael turned to her and said, 'You're not really watching this, are you? What's up?'

'It's nothing,' Kim said. 'Just a work thing playing on my mind.'

Michael gave her a sympathetic look. 'Oh dear,' he said. 'I've had a few of those. Is there anything you can do to sort it out before tomorrow?'

Kim, who'd been slumped in the settee, felt a sudden burst of energy surge through her. Immediately she sprang from her seat. 'Michael,' she said, 'you're a genius.'

'Where are you going?' he said as she made a sprint for the door.

'Nowhere. Just out.'

'Kim!' Ellen Murphy cracked open the door wide enough for Kim to absorb in one glance her beige hall, with its oatmeal runner, pale walls and bleached wooden bannisters.

She'd walked here rather than get in the car, hoping the exercise would go some way to calming the vicious angry beast clawing at her insides to escape. But the sight of Ellen Murphy hovering in her doorway displaying her neat little figure and her inoffensive older woman's hairstyle simply added more fuel to the beast. Kim had never felt violent to anyone in her life before, but right now she could have gone for Ellen Murphy's throat.

As if she'd read Kim's mind, Ellen put her hand to that very spot protectively. 'How did you get my address?' she said.

'I'm a police officer,' Kim said. 'And actually, your address isn't the only thing I found out about you.'

'Oh.' Ellen popped her head out of the door and looked this way and that. It was a bit late to start worrying about what the neighbours were thinking, Kim mused.

'Look, I can explain,' Ellen said, her tone cajoling.

'Save it,' snapped Kim.

'If you'd just come inside, then I could explain.'

'What I have to say can be said out here on the doorstep,' Kim said. 'And it's this. You are not fit to lick my father's boots, do you hear me? So when I've gone, what you are going to do is sit down and write him a letter and tell him you've been two-timing him, and that you're sorry, but now's the time to call it off because you've chosen the other man.'

Ellen gasped. 'I can't do that,' she said.

'You can. And you will.'

A whey-faced Ellen gripped the door handle tight, her knuckles white with the pressure of trying to stop them shaking. For her part, Kim couldn't have cared less how frightened she was. Any woman who hurt her lovely dad deserved any amount of suffering, was all she could think.

'Been nice knowing you, Ellen,' she said, turning to go. 'Have a nice life with

Douglas Burgess.'

As she strode down the driveway, she heard the door shut quietly behind her. Job done, she thought. And then a second thought occurred to her. She'd always thought she and her sister were chalk and cheese, she being the rational one and Shannon the one who could always be relied on to open her mouth before engaging her brain. Well, after tonight's little exhibition, maybe the two of them weren't so different after all.

★   ★   ★

Storm stood in the kitchen of Owl Cottage, waiting for the kettle to boil. Diana had sounded so excited when Storm had rung her to invite her round. She couldn't think of anything she'd rather do than spend the evening discussing her novel with Storm, she said, her effusiveness down the phone almost palpable.

That novel of Diana's. It was exquisite. So exquisite it pained her to think that anyone else could have written it apart from herself. *She herself* was the writer. *She herself* was the teacher. Not mousey little Diana Corbett who'd left school at sixteen and worked all her life in local government.

'I just sat down and wrote it,' she'd told Storm on one of those evenings when she'd kept her behind. 'Sometimes I think it wrote itself.'

How could writing be so effortless? It had never been like that for Storm. And recently it had got even harder. Today there'd been another text message from Tina. The publishers were expecting the proofs for the next novel. When could she expect them? the message had demanded. How could she possibly tell her that all she had so far was a blank page?

No one would know it wasn't hers. Not if she was careful. A few name changes here and there, some other details changed. After all, there were only seven basic plots, wasn't that what all the books on writing said? God knew she'd read enough of them, searching for the kind of inspiration that seemed to have fallen into Diana Corbett's scrawny little lap.

'And you haven't ever shown it anyone?' Storm had asked her after she'd read the manuscript herself.

'Absolutely not,' had come the reply. 'There's no one else whose opinion I value as much as yours.'

Maybe it was with these words the first seeds were sown. Storm turned her attention to the tray. It looked lovely, dressed as it was with those china cups she'd found hidden at the back of the cupboard and the silver teapot etched with a pastoral scene. Personally she'd have preferred something stiffer than tea, but her guest was teetotal. A medical condition, was all she'd say.

Someone was ringing the doorbell. Her visitor was here. Storm hurried to the door. As she passed the hall mirror, she caught a glimpse of her face — eager, full of anticipation. She needed to show more gravitas.

Diana was still under the delusion that her novel was only mediocre, and Storm needed to make sure she kept on thinking that way. She couldn't have her sending it off to some random agent because her writing teacher had told her she had talent, could she? That novel was Storm's. If she couldn't have Douglas, then she'd opt for fame and fortune instead.

★   ★   ★

Once again, Kim, as the more experienced officer, had been teamed up with Sally Hardman. This was the first night of their eight-day night shift, after a break of two days, and both were eager to get on with it. When the car radio crackled into life, Kim and Sally exchanged glances of eager anticipation.

'Officers required to attend at Owl Cottage, Lenton Wood,' the operator said. 'Someone's just reported a serious incident. Ambulance already in attendance.'

The two women looked at each other, aghast. Kim didn't know what she'd been expecting — perhaps a fight outside Lolita's, a local nightclub renowned for trouble. Maybe even a domestic. But Owl Cottage!

Without asking for further details or even consulting Sally, she informed the operator they were on their way. Not that Sally looked like she had any objections, if the force with which she put her foot down was anything to go by. To Kim's eyes, it looked like the adrenaline was beginning to pump through Sally's veins with the same intensity it was starting to pump through her own.

As they drove towards Lenton Wood, Kim's imagination went into overdrive. Dammit, they should have held Douglas Burgess in custody while they had the chance, she couldn't help thinking.

'Any more details?' she asked the operator.

'All I know is the first call to 999 was from a woman called Storm Costello, clearly upset, asking for an ambulance and the police too because, and I quote, 'Something's happened in my living room and I think I may have accidentally killed someone.'

* * *

The blue flashing light of the ambulance bathed the street outside Owl Cottage in a ghostly light. Kim recognised Noel Harper's car parked nearby at a crazy angle. He swung his long legs onto the ground just as Kim and Sally were getting out of their own car. Noel saw them immediately and headed towards them. But just before they came together, a second patrol car came swinging round the corner, all blues and twos, and out jumped Shaun Brennan and Todd Cameron, his partner.

'Looks like the cavalry's arrived,' Sally muttered under her breath. 'Typical!'

The two officers came striding over, reaching them at exactly the same moment Noel did.

'You two may as well be on your way,' Noel said, addressing Shaun. 'Kim here's familiar with this place, so . . .'

'Fair enough.' Shaun turned to the two women and gave them one of those inscrutable nods of acknowledgement that Sally seemed to find so infuriating.

As they watched him slope off back to his car, deep in conversation with his partner, Sally, unable to contain her delight at the sight of Shaun being given what she saw as the brush-off, flashed a wide grin at Kim.

The thought flashed through Kim's mind that there was a definite downside to Sally's youthful enthusiasm. This almost childish compulsion of hers to score points was one. Perhaps only time would teach her that you didn't have rivals in this job, only colleagues. Colleagues who, in times of need, would have your back. She hoped it wouldn't be a lesson she'd learn the hard way.

'So what's happened?' she asked Noel.

'All we know is this,' Noel said, 'victim's name is Diana Corbett.'

Sally and Kim exchanged shocked glances. 'You're joking!' they said in unison.

'I wish I was.'

'So this is nothing to do with Burgess, then?' Kim said.

'Not as far as I've been told.'

'I don't believe it!'

'Me neither,' Sally said.

Noel fixed her with a quizzical look, whereupon Kim explained her part in the affair of Diana and her neighbour, Hilda Rudge.

'Kim's been filling me in about this business between Storm Costello and Diana Corbett,' Sally said. 'I know for a fact Corbett's got form for trying to get a bit too close to those who don't particularly want to get that close to her.'

There she was again, this time trying to get Noel on her side. In Noel's favour, he wasn't biting.

'Look, we can stand here all day speculating,' he said. 'Let's just go inside and find out, shall we?'

* * *

Diana Corbett wasn't visible from the living room door due to the cluster of paramedics working on her. One of them glanced up and signalled with a barely noticeable shake of the head that it didn't look good for her.

Storm, apparently, was in the kitchen being given tea by another of the paramedics. Noel signalled to Kim to go with him. Once again, Storm was dressed in the billowing kaftan she'd been wearing the day Kim had paid her first visit to Owl Cottage. She was perched on a high stool, clutching a mug of something. Her two black eyes suggested she'd been crying.

'Now, then, Miss Costello,' Noel said, 'what's all this?'

His sympathetic manner only made the tears come again. It took a while, but eventually they managed to piece Storm's story together. She'd had a call from Diana Corbett, she said — a woman in her writing group, she explained. Unnecessarily, since they both knew who she was.

'She invited herself round even though I told her I was far too busy to have guests,' Storm said.

'Is she a friend of yours?' Noel asked.

'Good God, no! She said she was working on a short story for a competition and she wanted me to read what she'd written so far. I asked her to email it, but she said her laptop had died and she'd written the story by hand.' She'd been staring at her toenails — pink tonight — all the time she spoke. Now she lifted her eyes and met Kim's gaze pleadingly. 'She's a nuisance, Officer. But she's a lonely old woman. I thought if I invited her round, gave her tea, read her stuff and gave her some feedback, then she'd go back home satisfied.'

'Except that's not how it ended,' Kim said.

Storm raised her hands to her face and covered her eyes. 'She wanted me to be honest in my criticism. So I was. I tried to be kind of course, but the poor woman . . . Well, when it comes to her writing, she's delusional.'

'How did she end up on the floor, Storm?' Noel said.

Storm's bottom lip began to shake. 'I couldn't bear to look at her face any longer. Didn't want to listen to her going on and on about how much work she'd put into that tedious little story. But I couldn't get away from her.' Diana was becoming more and more aggressive, accusing her of simply failing to understand her work, and calling her stupid, Storm said. 'She said such hurtful things. My books were old hat. No one was reading them anymore.' She wouldn't

271

stop, Storm said, and the abuse got worse. 'It was frightening, the way it just kept tumbling from the mouth of such a small inoffensive-looking woman,' she went on.

'Ms Costello,' Noel said, holding up his hand in warning, 'I have to tell you now that if you're about to confess to attacking Miss Corbett, then I must caution you.'

Storm looked at him, aghast. 'No!' she exclaimed. 'Of course I didn't. What do you take me for?' All she'd been about to tell him was that she'd turned her back on Diana, she said. 'Her face was white with fury. There was spittle flying from her lips. I just needed to shut her out. I turned round, picked up the poker from the fireside companion, and started poking the fire.' She glanced plaintively at Noel, then Kim, then back at Noel again. 'It was just something to do with my hands, you know, to drown her nonsense out.'

And that, apparently, was when Diana hurled herself at Storm's back.

'I spun round and raised the poker. It was in self-defence,' she said.

'And did you strike her with it?' Noel asked.

'No!'

'So she just fell down then? Of her own accord?' The sarcasm dripped from Noel's voice.

'I may have put out my other hand. The one not holding the poker,' Storm said. 'I wanted to stop her getting any closer. But then she just sort of crumpled and fell down at my feet.'

'Ms Costello,' Noel said, his voice suddenly solemn, 'I'd like you to come with us to the station where we can take some samples. Would you give your permission for us to do that?'

'Samples?' Storm looked confused.

'DNA,' Kim whispered. 'And we need to examine the clothes you were wearing at the time of the incident. These, presumably.'

Storm nodded, her face a ghastly white.

'I'll come upstairs with you so you can get changed into something else, okay?'

Again, Storm nodded, but seemed reluctant to put one foot in front of the other. In a bid to get her moving, Kim took her arm. A knock at the door stopped her mid-gesture. It was one of the paramedics.

'I'm sorry,' the paramedic said. 'There was nothing more we could do.'

Storm gave a little gasp. Noel and Kim exchanged a solemn glance.

'I think it's time to get the CSIs in here,' he said solemnly. 'Until we know the results of the PM, I'm declaring this a crime scene.'

★ ★ ★

Kim was sitting at the table in Dad's living room, only half-listening to Shannon as she read the story of the incident at Owl Cottage out loud. Kim wished she'd just shut up. Dad wasn't even pretending to listen. He just stared into space, lost in his own thoughts. And as for herself, well, she knew the story back to front and inside out.

From Owl Cottage, Kim had accompanied Storm to the station, taken a DNA samples, got her a coffee, then sat with her while they waited for her solicitor, who seemed none too ecstatic at being dragged out of bed in the middle of the night.

When her shift ended, she went back home and tried to grab some sleep, though in the end that proved impossible. All she could think about were the events of the evening.

'Said Peter Morley, solicitor to Storm Costello, 'At no stage was my client charged either with assault or the murder of Diana Corbett',' Shannon continued to read. ''It has been confirmed that Miss Corbett, who suffered from a severe heart condition, died of a heart attack while at the home of the author.''

'Yeah, okay, Shannon,' Kim said irritably. 'This is old news. She's out. She's free. That's her face smiling all over the front page, next to her husband.'

She'd seen the photo herself in one of the nationals, though she'd chosen not to read any further than the caption. *CLOSER THAN EVER AFTER TRAUMATIC EVENT*, it had read. Two smug faces staring out at the camera. How was Diana coping with that? she wondered.

First there were two men in her life, then there were none. It was kind of the opposite of buses.

Shannon looked up from the paper.

'What's the matter with you?' she said. 'I thought you'd enjoy reading about something you had a part in.'

'Well I don't.'

Dad rose from his chair and went into the kitchen. Probably just to get out of the way. He hated bickering.

'He's worse than you. All he does is sit there moping,' Shannon said. 'He's been like that for a month now. Ever since he stopped seeing that Diana. Although he's well shot of her if you ask me.'

Kim wished she could agree. It was what she'd intended after all, when she'd gone marching round to Diana Corbett's house, ordering her to break it off with her dad. Had she known then what it would do to him, she never would have made that visit. It was if he was right back in that time again, just after mum died, when he could find no joy in anything.

'She's got another book coming out

soon, it says here,' Shannon said. ''Hot on the heels of her current novel, *A Person of Interest*, Storm's new novel, *A Work of Fiction*, will be out in the autumn.'

'Well, I hope it's better than her last,' muttered Kim. 'Now, can we change the subject?'

★   ★   ★

'Why don't you want to come with me to the book launch?'

It was six months later and Storm Costello — by way of making up to Michael for missing her last gig at the library — had decided to hold her launch there. So that all those friends and neighbours and in particular her writing group, who'd staunchly stood by her after the unfortunate business with poor Diana, could attend, was how she'd put it. The thought of bumping into Ellen Murphy after the way she'd attacked her was just too much for Kim. It would be far better if she stayed away.

'If I tell you, you'll hate me,' Kim mumbled.

'Try me,' Michael said.

So Kim did. To give him credit, Michael listened patiently without one word of interruption.

'So that's it,' she said. 'Because I forced her to write to Dad and confess she was two-timing him, it made Dad really unhappy for ages.'

Michael furrowed his brow while he thought about what she said. 'But you did right, Kim. It would have come out sooner or later. How would he have felt if he'd found out you knew that Ellen had been two-timing him and you hadn't said anything?'

'He'd have killed me.'

'Exactly. Anyway, think about it this way. If she hadn't dumped him, he never would have brought Compton back from the rescue centre.'

Kim smiled. Ah yes, Compton, the cross-breed with the big heart and the even bigger paws. Now there was a creature who would never let a man down. 'I just wanted him to happy,' she

278

said. 'And I thought I could fix it for him.'

Michael went over to her and rested his arms on her shoulders. 'You know what this is all about, don't you, this self-loathing?' he said. 'You hate yourself for doing exactly what Shannon would have done.'

He was right of course.

'Have you told her what you did?' he asked her.

'You're joking, aren't you? I'd never hear the end of it.'

Michael chuckled. 'Look,' he said, 'the only way you're going to get over this is to come with me to the launch. Face your demons. Though I bet any money Ellen Murphy won't even be there.'

'How do you mean?'

'Think about it. Storm and Douglas are back together again. Do you really think she'll want to see them playing happy couples all night long?' He brushed the top of Kim's head with a kiss. 'Now get your coat. We've got thirty minutes tops before the wine runs out.'

★　★　★

The book launch was coming to an end. There had been speeches — an effusive one from Storm thanking everyone for their support — especially Douglas, of course, who raised his glass in acknowledgement, followed by a lengthy, even more gushing one from a woman called Tina who said she was Storm's agent.

Kim had been listening to all this with Michael at her side and a glass of tepid white wine in her hand, while scanning the crowd for Ellen Murphy. Now that she could finally be sure Ellen wasn't there, she felt able to relax.

'I think I ought to grab a copy and get in the queue,' Michael said. 'Being as it's my library sort of thing.'

Kim rolled her eyes. Michael was a stickler for obligation. A long queue was forming at the desk where Storm, obviously enjoying being the centre of attention, was busy signing copies of her book. At this rate, she was going to have a long wait for him. Once she was alone, she took out her phone to check if Dad had been in touch. He had — with another snap of Compton carrying one of

Dad's shoes in his mouth — and saw she had a missed call from an unknown number. Intrigued, she rang it. It was Ellen Murphy.

'I know I must be the last person you want to hear from, Kim, and I understand that perfectly,' she said. 'But please, hear me out. I'm ringing you because you're police and I think I've just discovered something that's very, very illegal.'

'What is it, Ellen?'

'I've got Storm's latest novel here,' she said. 'I didn't want to come to the launch for obvious reasons, so I pre-ordered it online. And, well, I'm one hundred percent sure she didn't write it.'

'How do you mean?'

'I mean it's Diana's novel. Not exactly word for word — she's changed a few names and such — but the plot's the same as I remember it when she showed me a draft.'

'Are you sure about this?'

'My copy came yesterday, and I read it straight through cover to cover,' she said. 'I've had all night to think about it. And I'm not wrong.'

She'd befriended Diana after finding herself sitting next to her at one of the few sessions of Storm's writing classes she'd attended, she said. Diana was keen to make a friend, since she knew no one locally, and seemed to have picked on Ellen, who'd felt sorry for her and invited her round to hers for tea a couple of times as well as accepting reciprocal invitations.

'All this was before Doug and I properly got together,' she said, her embarrassment leeching down the line. 'I'm afraid I dropped her after that. Life got too complicated.'

Unsurprisingly, with two men on the go, Kim couldn't help thinking.

'Are you still there?' Ellen's voice interrupted her train of thought.

'Yes. Tell me. What format was Ellen's novel in? A hard copy?'

'No. It was on her laptop. She didn't have a printer. I read at least ten chapters while she was in the kitchen getting a meal ready for the two of us one night.' There was a pause. 'Actually, she didn't really show it me. In fact, she never knew

I'd read it,' she added. 'She really wouldn't have liked it if she'd found out I'd been poking around in her stuff.'

This woman really was a piece of work, Kim thought. Oh yes, she'd definitely done the right thing warning her off her dad.

'Ellen,' Kim said, putting her personal feelings aside, 'are you prepared to stand up in a court of law and say what you've just told me?'

'Of course.'

'In that case, I'm going to have to interrupt Storm's book-signing and make an arrest,' she said. 'What you've just told me puts a whole new light on things.'

★ ★ ★

'Perverting the course of justice' was how they'd described what she'd done. Considering she'd tampered with those brake cables herself — a trick she'd picked up from her old trustworthy bedside companion, *How to Murder Your Characters* — and the only person hurt was herself, she thought it grossly unfair of the judge to sentence her.

The man had a heart of steel, obviously. There he sat, with that stupid wig perched on top of his head, while she poured her heart out to the court. Confessed to all and sundry that when she'd found out her husband was having an affair, all she'd wanted to do was die.

Yes, okay, maybe she *had* wanted it to look like Douglas had tampered with the brakes and caused her death, and maybe that hadn't been very nice of her. But really, could anyone blame her? Obviously this particular judge could, otherwise she wouldn't be where she was now, forced to share this grim little cell with a woman who hadn't paid her TV licence.

It could have been longer though, her sojourn at Her Majesty's Pleasure. A lot longer. But thanks to poor Diana's dodgy ticker giving out the moment Storm wrestled her laptop out of her puny arms, she'd literally got away with murder. There'd been no need in the end to connect the poker with Diana's head. Being quite a squeamish person, she hadn't been looking forward to that bit much at all.

Stealing Diana's novel had cost her her career, though, and maybe that was the worst thing. Worse even than losing Douglas. Tina had dropped her like hot coals. Told her she'd make sure she never got another agent again.

If only she'd been more careful and got rid of the evidence. But she thought she'd got away with it, and that Diana dropping down dead her feet so conveniently, leaving her novel behind on her laptop, meant she was free from scrutiny.

But she hadn't reckoned on someone else having read a good-sized chunk of Diana's book and blabbing about to the police. Naturally they decided to search for the laptop at her house. And when they couldn't find it there, where else would they come but to Owl Cottage? And that was where they'd found it. Tucked away in her knicker drawer. Such humiliation!

She'd got an eighteen-month stretch in front of her. How on earth was she going to fill it? If she asked nicely, would they let her have some pens and paper? Perhaps she could write a memoir. There was bound to be masses of material in a place like this. Forget agents; she could self-publish. That was the growing thing now, wasn't it? Or so she'd heard.

You had to make your own luck in this world. And there was no time like the present.

THE LATE MRS. FIVE

Richard Wormser

Soon after Paul Porter arrives in the small rural town of Lowndesburg, he is shocked to see his beautiful ex-wife Edith getting into an expensive limousine. He discovers she is now married to rich landowner John Hilliard the Fifth, to whose mansion he makes a visit hoping to sell agricultural machinery, only to find nobody home. But the local police know of his visit — and when they discover Edith's dead body there, he becomes the prime suspect as the slayer of the late Mrs. Five!

LORD JAMES HARRINGTON AND THE SPRING MYSTERY

Lynn Florkiewicz

James and his wife Beth are hosting the annual spring fair when wealthy recluse Delphine Brooks-Hunter is murdered. While James is summoned to the reading of her will and is tasked with solving an intriguing riddle, Beth tackles her own mystery after discovering a homeless man suffering from amnesia. As they delve deeper, a number of questions emerge. What links Delphine to the fairground folk? Who would harm such a refined lady? Are rumours of wartime espionage true? As they unravel the truth, they uncover more than they bargained for . . .

LORD JAMES HARRINGTON AND THE SUMMER MYSTERY

Lynn Florkiewicz

It's summer, and the annual tennis tournament between Cavendish and Charnley is underway; but a sudden spate of jewel thefts prompts James to put his sleuthing hat on. His investigation suggests that the criminals are using an ancient smuggling network. Can he convince his good friend, DCI George Lane, of his suspicions? Is the murder of the tennis umpire connected? Could a long-term resident really be a criminal mastermind? James desperately struggles for answers as he explores hidden tunnels, studies old maps and examines the motives of his fellow villagers.